Praise for *The Complicated Calculus (and Cows) of Carl Paulsen*

"Carl Paulsen cannot be budged. He misses his mom, he wants to keep his cows, and he thinks Andy Olnan is cuter than cute—cuter than his 'another' by a long shot. Even as he's pushed, pulled, and asked to change his mind by those around him—including Andy—Carl stays true to who he is. We can all take a lesson (or several) from that strength and resilience. A great read."

–Kirstin Cronn-Mills, author of *Beautiful Music for Ugly Children* and *Original Fake*

"Gary Eldon Peter's debut novel, *The Complicated Calculus (and Cows) of Carl Paulsen,* is what great young adult fiction should be. It's brilliant, beautiful, and brave—the sort of story that grabs you by the hand and pulls you forward, page after page, until you reach the end and finally take a breath. There's nothing complicated about it: this is a great novel."

–Bryan Bliss, National Book Award longlisted author of *We'll Fly Away*

"In this engrossing coming-of-age story, Carl, a teenager living with his family on a Minnesota dairy farm grapples with first love, the loss of his mother, and his distanced relationship with his father. Peter's intimate and nuanced portrayal of Carl's romantic feelings for the charismatic and mysterious new student, Andy, and the hopes Carl has for a more authentic connection with those around him is deeply honest and endearing. An inspiring story about the courage it takes to be your whole self no matter what."

–Veera Hiranandani, author of the Newbery Honor winning *The Night Diary*

"Meet Carl Paulsen—he's not rich, urban, or 'fabulous.' He's a farm boy devoted to his cows, his younger sister, and his widowed father (in that order). When Carl meets Andy Olnan, the new boy in town, everything suddenly changes, just like that moment in *West Side Story* when Maria meets Tony. I absolutely loved this fresh, unpredictable, and heartrending-but-hopeful book. Funny, sad, closeted farm kid Carl Paulsen is my new best friend."

—Brian Malloy, author of *The Year of Ice* and *After Francesco*

"With insight and grace, Gary Eldon Peter explores the big questions: Who am I? Who will I be? And who will I let truly know me? This novel's gentleness is underlain with the absolute determination of a quiet teenager's quest for self-identity."

—Alison McGhee, author of *Where We Are* and *What I Leave Behind*

"Carl Paulsen wants to belong to this world, broken though it may be. There is a magic in this book, magic that makes us feel we are in this young man's heart as he struggles to find his place in the world. The words shimmer with gentle, heartbreaking empathy. The result is a beautiful piece of fiction, sure to make anyone who reads it feel less alone."

—N. West Moss, author of *Flesh and Blood* and *The Subway Stops at Bryant Park*

"Fearlessly exploring the nuances of love and friendship, Peter's characters navigate life's inevitable disappointments with humor and hope. Teenagers will love this story of vulnerability and courage as Carl finds the strength to act on his own feelings, and subsequently realizes his family and friends' love for him is profoundly rooted in acceptance."

—Carol Dines, author of *This Distance We Call Love* and *The Queen's Soprano*

"Whoever you are, wherever you're from, get ready to fall in love with Carl Paulsen. Gary Eldon Peter's hero is smart, charming, modest (but opinionated where it counts) and, speaking of falling in love, he's gay. A new boy at school catches Carl's eye and seems to return his interest. Or does he? Carl's roller-coaster of a semester is warmly familiar and yet full of surprising twists and turns. This book will have huge appeal across age groups and backgrounds."

–David Pratt, author of *Wallaçonia*

"Once I picked up *The Complicated Calculus (and Cows) of Carl Paulsen*, I had a hard time putting it down. I fell hard for Carl and his very active but pragmatic imagination, his sense of irony and humor, his clear-eyed view of the world. And he does love his cows!"

–Judith Katz, author of *The Escape Artist* and *Running Fiercely Toward a High Thin Sound*

THE COMPLICATED CALCULUS (AND COWS) OF CARL PAULSEN

Gary Eldon Peter

Fitzroy Books

Published by Fitzroy Books,
An imprint of
Regal House Publishing, LLC
Raleigh, NC 27605
All rights reserved

ISBN -13 (paperback): 9781646032532
ISBN -13 (epub): 9781646032549
Library of Congress Control Number: 2021943790

Interior and cover design by Lafayette & Greene
Cover images © by C. B. Royal

Regal House Publishing, LLC
https://regalhousepublishing.com

Printed in the United States of America

For my parents, my sister Karen, and for BL

1

MILK

It's the official start of tenth grade, and everyone is texting and talking at the same time, even though the person they're texting is probably less than ten feet away. But if you can do both, and do them well, your coolness quotient is obviously very high. Mine, I'm afraid, is in the negative digits, but then again it probably always has been.

And on and on with the summer pictures: for the C group, trips to the Black Hills or the Wisconsin Dells; for the kids next up the ladder, Disney World, out west somewhere like a bunch of national parks, or maybe California; for the ultra rich, even farther. Sue Tilford—her father is president of the Fullerton Savings and Loan and has lent my father lots of money to keep our farm going—went to a fancy summer camp in France to learn to speak the language so she'd be ready for some equally fancy college in a few years, and a group of girls from the first two groups crowd around her like she's a rock star, oohing and aahing over her pictures of the actual Eiffel Tower. And there are plenty of other pictures of places closer to home: lots of tanning on the raft at Woodland Lake in between shifts at the Dairy Queen or the canning factory, or after hot July days walking soybean fields to weed out the corn that isn't supposed to be there but that always manages to get mixed up with the soybean seeds.

I don't have a cell phone, and will probably never get one unless I can talk my father into joining the twenty-first century or I find some way to pay for it myself. *Too expensive, Too expensive,* my father says whenever I ask for one, *and besides which this whole texting insanity is destroying what little there is left of the English language, not to mention the destruction of face to face social discourse,* whatever that is. As a former high school English teacher he is very concerned about such things, and I should be too because some day, he says, the world would belong to me.

I don't want the world, at least not all of it, but it doesn't matter. There is no one I want to text anyway. If there were someone I wanted to talk to, I would do it in person. That would please my father to no end. But for now, more than anything I just want my piece of paper telling me where to be the Tuesday after Labor Day, the first day of school, what my locker combination is, what teachers I'll have to endure five days a week for the next nine months.

And even if I did have a cell phone, I wouldn't have any pictures to show. *There are no vacations when you own a dairy farm,* my father says, and often. *It's twenty-five hours a day, eight days a week, 366 days a year.*

And then he waits to see if I get the joke, even though our life is anything but. There is a lot to worry about—milk prices (more often down than up); the takeover by the "big guys" (farmers who sat behind desks as if they were the president of IBM and who let the Vet Science grads from Iowa State or the U of Minnesota in color-coordinated overalls milk the 350 head herd); money, and a lot of it, borrowed to keep us going (my father explaining for the umpteenth time, when I asked why we couldn't get cable like everyone else on the planet, how a mortgage worked and me rolling my eyes to let him know that, yes, I *did* know what a mortgage was, and that, yes, I was well aware that we were way behind on ours).

He could have also added that there aren't many friends either, at least not the human kind. With a small operation like ours (around twenty cows, more when the calves come) it's the "girls," as my mother liked to call them, who are your friends. You see them everyday, they have names, and you worry about what kind of day she's having.

No.

Not friends.

Family.

I could make excuses that when you're the only boy in the

family on a dairy farm that feels like it could go under at any moment, and you're working all the time, and add to that school nine months of the year, having a lot of friends—human ones at least—isn't at the top of the to-do list. And just to make the story a little more grim, besides chores there's my three-year-old little sister to take care of, and since my mother died I have to spend a lot more time with my father since he's the only parent I have left.

But those things really aren't true. My father hired the daughter of a neighbor, Ellen Hansen, to live with us and take care of Anna. And I haven't been spending any more time with my father than I did when my mother was alive. The only difference is that there are more awkward silences between us because she's no longer there to fill them up. In other words, farm kids, even dairy farm kids, can have friends just like anybody else. It just takes a little more work.

And in my case, while I don't want to make it sound like I'm making excuses—and I hate the expression *it's complicated* more than I can say—it's complicated. Being gay, and as far as I know being the only gay person in this entire school (likely not the case, but it may as well be) adds another...dimension to things, as my mother used to like to say. *Dimension* was one of her favorite words. She could find dimension in anything: food, the color of the sky, even our cows. When one of her girls wasn't giving much milk, or seemed unwell, she'd say, "Well, she's in another dimension it seems. She'll come back to us." And she usually did.

Not that I go around broadcasting all of my "dimensions," but I'm sure a lot of people have figured it out. Some probably think it's the worst thing in the world, some might think it's totally cool, some probably don't care much either way. I'd like to think that, what with being well into the new millennium and awareness of diversity and all that, you could be gay at this school and it might be okay. You probably wouldn't meet the boy of your dreams but at least people would leave you alone.

But this is Fullerton, Minnesota, population 2,076, according to the sign on the edge of town. It seems a lot smaller. And

even though we're only an hour and a half away from the big
city (Minneapolis), we may as well be on Jupiter in 1965. There's
no gay pride parade in the summer, no gay bar (and even if
there was, I'd be too young to get in anyway), no groups for
parents to talk about their gay kids. If it's gay anything you're
after, prepare to take a road trip, and in my case, not only is
there no phone, there's no license yet, and even if I do get one,
no car unless my dad lets me borrow the pickup, no questions
asked. Good luck with that one.

So there you are. Or where I am.

I can't wait for the day when I can get away and start my
real life, but then again, if I think too hard about it, leaving the
cows seems unbearable. Sure, I'd miss Anna, but she'll eventually grow up, have a life. And my father too, I suppose, because
he's got to get on with his life, too, maybe meet somebody and
start over. But when I think about the cows and that moment
of my going, whenever that will be, it takes my breath away. I
can't explain why. The classic definition of a conundrum, my
father would say. It's one of his favorite words, which is saying
a lot given his previous life as an English teacher and all that
he has to choose from. *Everyone needs farmers but the government
bends over backward to make it as difficult as possible to be one. You try
to do the right thing by feeding the earth but you're the one who's going to
end up starving.* So that was it in a nutshell (one of my father's
most hated clichés, but it was true): his life, my life, our life…
one big conundrum. It sounded like a disease to me, but one
with no cure.

Someone taps me on the shoulder. "Excuse me, but is this the
line for sophomores to register?"

I turn around. "Yup." I know immediately that this boy,
just because of his ridiculous question, is new. Anyone who's
been in Fullerton for even just a year or two knows that this
is how we do things, though why they couldn't just mail the
stupid schedules, or email them, or text them (talk about not
knowing your audience), is beyond me. But this ritual has gone
on for decades; my parents did the same thing when they were

at Fullerton High. Besides that, he isn't bent over a phone, his thumbs going a mile a minute. And he's making eye contact, another lost art my father has been mourning. And I'm making it too because, as my father says, that's the whole point. Someone looks at you, you look at them, it's how humans connect and size each other up. It doesn't count unless both people are doing it. I decide against going into my whole spiel about how this isn't really registration because you're not really registering for anything, it's already been decided, it's just a ploy to get everybody in one place before the semester begins, but why exactly is beyond me. Why confuse the new guy?

"Thought so."

And so we stand there, looking at each other, and then looking at the floor, then at each other again. I can hear my father in my head: *looking away is cheating.* Maybe this guy's dad has told him the same thing.

"I'm Andy. Andy Olnan." He puts his hand out.

"Carl. Carl Paulsen."

My father taught me to shake hands at a very early age, when my tiny fingers would get swallowed up in the sweaty palms of adults like our church minister (when we used to go) or other farmers we'd run into at the feed store in town. *Firmly,* he'd said. *There's nothing worse than shaking hands with a dead fish.* That, and make sure you look them in the eye while you're doing it. Firmness! Eye contact! You had to have both. But this is the first time I've ever shaken hands with someone my own age. I didn't know it was done, as dumb as that sounds. Sure, I'd seen guys in school doing high fives or elaborate fist bump routines that you needed a five-page diagram to learn how to figure out, but hardly ever a straightforward, no-frills grown-up handshake.

It seems like he holds on to me for longer than you're supposed to, but that could have been my imagination. I'd never paid attention to the length of handshakes before.

His hand is a lot smoother than mine, my first clue that he couldn't be a farm kid. No matter how hard you scrubbed, or how much of your mother's hand cream that you slathered on, you couldn't get rid of that roughness. And that was good, my mother said, because it reminded you of who you were and where you came from. But now it only embarrasses me, the scratchiness of my fingers against his, which feel soft and paper-thin.

Finally he lets go, or maybe I did first. It's hard to tell.

With the handshake moment out of the way, and as we stand there waiting for either the line to move or for one of us to do or say something, I take a quick inventory.

Clothing choices: a plain white T-shirt, blue jeans, slightly faded and a bit tight, and cowboy boots. If the hands aren't a giveaway, the clothes are. Definitely NOT a farm kid. It's the cowboy boots. There's not one speck of dirt on them. It's not that farm kids don't wear cowboy boots (though I don't—too uncomfortable), but his look like he just bought them on the way here and wore them out of the store. He's definitely never worn them while mucking out stalls or milking; you could use the tops of them as a mirror for combing your hair. Wearing cowboy boots for the coolness factor, rather than for practicality—typical town kid move.

Body type: about the same height as me and slender like me, but more...wiry. Probably a lot stronger than he looked. Not from farm work, though; maybe he worked out or maybe he was just born that way. Lucky him. I had always thought working on a farm would fill me out, maybe even give me some muscle—there had to be some advantages to living this way—but nope. I seem to get skinnier as I get older, when it should be the other way around. It was a combination of metabolism and worry, my mother said. *You worry too much for a child,* she would say, when I asked about a sick cow or our money problems, which I seemed to know about without being told. *You'll have lots of time to worry when you grow up. If you don't stop worrying, you're going to dry up and blow away.* The idea of that both scared me and made me laugh, the thought of being like a husk of corn, floating, but to where?

Hair: blond and completely straight, and way longer than my father would have ever allowed me to have. Long enough for him to be able to flip it back with a quick nod of his head, or to comb through it with his fingers, both of which he did over and over during the time we were standing there. It was probably such a habit he might not have even known he was doing it, but if I had hair like that, I'd make sure people knew about it too. Compared to him I looked like I'd just enlisted in the Marines, thanks to my father and his clippers (home haircuts a cost-saving measure instituted from the first time I needed a haircut as a toddler and which were still in effect, even though I asked over and over if I could please go to a regular barber like everyone else). Blond hair, too, and more curly, on his tanned forearms. Again, more than I had there too. A bit of stubble on his chin, enough to shave, if not every day. I wonder if he belonged with the seniors but had gotten in the wrong line.

Eyes: Green, or maybe blue-green. Was there even such a color? There was a hardness to them, like marbles. Squinty, like he either needs glasses or is sizing things up.

Of course I've been staring. But he's been staring too. Both of us busted.

He looks down at his paper. "You know what? I'm an O and you're a P. How about that."

I look at my paper, too, as if I somehow need confirmation that, yes, I am a P. "We'll probably be next to each other in classes if they do it alphabetically." When I look at him again, I try to gauge what he thinks about that, if it totally repulses him or is just okay, but it's just more squinting, which doesn't tell me anything. "But sometimes they don't do it that way, sometimes they do it randomly, or you can pick wherever you want to sit, or…"

I can't believe I'm standing there babbling on about seating charts, but maybe it's because I'm trying to say something, anything to keep him there before he disappears for good, even though that could not be more stupid since he's obviously going to be in school like everybody else. And because I can't say what I'd really like to say: *Sorry for all the staring at you but I think you're…what? Beautiful?* Cheesy beyond words and rather pathetic. But he is. And I'm back to how to hang on to this moment, on to him, because once we're all back and into the routine and people see him and meet him, he'll have moved way beyond me into the upper echelon. He was too, well, *beautiful* for that not to happen.

Then it's finally my turn at the stupid desk to pick up more papers and my locker combination, and he's up at the other desk next to mine doing the same thing. He turns and smiles and I smile back and then the cranky older woman with the cat-eye glasses (which would normally be quite retro on anyone else) is asking me to spell my dad's name one more time for her, and when I'm finally done, I turn around to look for him, but he's gone.

That night, in bed, though the whole conversation lasted probably three minutes tops, I can't sleep, because I'm replaying it over and over. Andy Olnan, whoever he is, is keeping me awake. Handshake, eyes, hair.

To put it another way—and this is embarrassing and I could never tell another living person about it ever—but when I think about meeting Andy Olnan I'm thinking about the beginning of *West Side Story,* one my mother's favorite movies which she had to watch whenever it came on TV, even though it was way too long and the ending made her cry. Tony, a Jet, and Maria, sister of a Shark, suddenly spot one another across the gym at the dance and everyone else disappears, and it's like they're in a dream. At least it was that way for me; I don't know about Andy. I hoped so.

So cheesy, I know, but I can't help it.

Another boy had never kept me awake before.

I don't mind it.

2

Goodness and Mercy

"Milking's done. I'll get back to painting the tool shed in a little bit, if that's okay."

I put my cereal bowl in the soapy water in the sink, give it a push, and wait for it to hit bottom. It's Friday morning, the beginning of the long Labor Day weekend, and with morning chores out of the way, I'm looking forward to some alone time in my room, maybe even a pre-lunchtime nap. It's summer vacation for only three more days, and I'm not ready to let go yet.

My father, sitting at the kitchen table, looks up from the newspaper he's spread out in front of him. "The cemetery. Remember?" He shakes his head. "How could you forget that?"

And yet somehow I have. Did that make me a terrible person?

We'd gone last year, on the first anniversary, and I knew without either of us saying anything, that we'd started a tradition. Of course we had. But had it really been a whole year? I remembered how slowly time seemed to move from when she died to that visit a year later, but how fast it had gone from a year ago to now.

We were getting used to her being gone. Or maybe it was just me who felt that way. Whether or not my father did, I couldn't say. We didn't talk about such things; why we didn't I couldn't say anything about that either. Sometimes it seems like there's an opening; we're watching TV and reminded of something she liked or said, but neither of us are able to do anything about it, or there's some distraction, like time for milking and chores, or Anna needing something or other, or just being too tired from everything to do much remembering.

But maybe that was the whole point of going, to somehow

make up for what we couldn't say or what we lost track of in those other moments. Society is governed by rituals. We learned that in geography class way back in the eighth grade, and here was one of our very own. But somehow that doesn't make me feel any better about forgetting.

Anna isn't going; she'll stay home with Ellen. She's too little to remember anyway, my father says. She'll come with us in a few years, when it'll mean something.

But before we can go we have to get dressed up, even though we'll just have to change back into chore clothes afterward. "The least we can do is look nice," my father says, sensing that I'm about to complain. And of course he's right, and once again I'm a terrible person for caring only about what a pain it is to have to put on a suit in the middle of a hot early September day instead of what it is we're trying to do: remember. Though never mind that my mother wouldn't care what we wore, she'd understand the comfort of stained T-shirts, jeans, the scuffed summer tennis shoes I wore from April to November. My father, however, will not be moved, so why try?

So we're out here now, standing in front of the small granite square with my mother's name on it and her dates, and my father's too, though there's a space there for his second date to come. The grass could stand a mowing, and it would be nice if someone got down there with some clippers so you see my mother's full name. But maybe that was our job, and we were neglecting it. It feels like we're orbiting about ten feet away from the sun and it's a million degrees, even though you would think by now things might be cooling off even just a little. I'm tugging at my shirt collar, scratchy and two sizes too small around my neck, and I'm trying to think about my mother and remember, but what to remember? There are too many things to remember and yet not enough, both at the same time. It's easier to think about Andy Olnan, about the other day and meeting him, and what will happen next week, when school starts. *I'm an O, and you're a P. How about that?* Yes, how about that. With my luck my teachers will probably decide that it's time to change things up:

let's seat everybody alphabetically by first name this year. Too many people in between, unless it worked out somehow that we ended up across from each other. Would that be better or worse than just being able to look at the back of his head? Too many glances, and the teacher might figure out that something is up. If I luck out and it's business as usual, I'd at least have his amazing hair to focus on.

My father, his head bowed, shoots me a sideways glare, as if he knows what I'm thinking—or not thinking—about. Then he closes his eyes and starts whispering something: *The Lord is my shepherd: I shall not want.* Psalm 23, my mother's favorite, and mine too, though that's because it's the only one that I really know. Psalm 24, 25, or 40 could be just as nice, but we'd never learned those in Sunday school.

I close my eyes and try to say the words, too, but nothing comes out. The back of my neck won't stop itching, and if I'm not scratching, I'm pulling on my sleeves, trying to make them longer. What if someone sees me? *Did you see that faggy Paulsen all dressed up out at the cemetery? What a loser.* I can see it in the *Fullerton Weekly Citizen* in the "Around Town" section:

> Locals Edwin Paulsen and son, Carl, fifteen, were spotted at Calvary Cemetery, noting the two-year anniversary of the passing of Vandeline Paulsen, Edwin's wife and mother of Carl and Anna, age three. Carl was seen in a suit purchased two years earlier, also worn at the funeral of the late Mrs. Paulsen. Falling milk prices have apparently prevented dairyman and former English teacher Paulsen, rumored to be in dire financial straits, from making necessary clothing purchases for his son, as the younger Paulsen's arms stuck out from the suit like a monkey's.

Within hours, if not minutes, word would get back to Andy Olnan that I was actually out in public looking like a complete and total moron and wearing a clip-on tie, no less. Andy might even be driving by on Highway 5 with his mother or father at this very moment and see it himself. Our friendship, or whatever more it might turn out to be, would be over before it had really begun.

When I open my eyes, I peer up at my father, who seems to know I'm looking at him and opens his eyes too. Instead of being angry he grins at me, as if we're sharing a little joke, and the two of us finish the psalm together. I like the low rumbling of our voices when we get to *Surely goodness and mercy shall follow me all the days of my life,* and it's hard for me to distinguish whose voice is whose.

My mother had been right. Not long before she'd gotten sick, she told me I was about to change, and I'd better be ready, because it was going to happen whether I liked it or not.

And now she's missing it.

Missing me.

We get to the *Amen* together, but mine feels stuck, the lump in my throat won't let it out.

The farther away from the cemetery we get, the smaller the lump becomes, and though I know this too makes me sound like a terrible person, I'm relieved that it's over, that we've done our duty for another year. He probably wouldn't admit it, but I have a feeling my father is glad too.

"I don't know about you, but I'm completely soaked." He wipes his forehead with his handkerchief, starts the pickup, and pulls onto the highway. "Eighty-five on the fifth of September." He shakes his head and laughs, like we'd just left a barbeque or something. "Wanna bet tomorrow night we'll have a frost?"

"Hm." His collar is soaked with sweat that's slowly making its way down the front of his shirt. I'm drenched, too, and I can feel it rolling down from the top of my chest to my stomach. Even though growing up with it, I should be used to the smell of manure by now; that, mixed with our sweat, is making me a little dizzy. I open the window for some fresh air, and I wonder about Andy Olnan's smell, and how it has to be entirely different than my own, mostly soap, hopefully, and not like he's taken a bath in that hideous Axe that a lot of the boys in my class have started wearing, one whiff of which has the potential to send me to the nurse's office with a migraine. I wish I'd taken a good sniff of him when I had the chance. I need to remember to do that, I think, when school starts, like it's another item on my to-do list: make sure I have a clean shirt to wear the first day; bring notebooks and pencils; find Andy Olnan and smell him as soon as possible.

A mile from home, my father slows down so he can get a better look at Reggie Davidson's corn. "Will you look at that," he says. "Lots of green there. And I'm not just talking about the color. Damn." He shakes his head. "God-*damn*."

Every time we drive by their place, my father curses Reggie for buying the land, and then himself for not beating Reggie to it when he had the chance, not long after he and my mother were married. My mother would try to get him to let go of it, but he wouldn't. "What an idiot I was," he'd say, tapping his forehead for emphasis. "Now we couldn't afford to buy an acre of it. But, nope, we had to stick with dairy."

Though he never said so and would probably deny it if you asked him, but missing out was my mother's doing, who said we were smart to keep things small, as her parents had done, focus on one thing, not try compete by growing corn and soybeans too. "If we wanted to go big, we should have had more children," she'd say, laughing. But there was just me, who didn't appear until both of them were close to thirty, then a long time before Anna came along, and she was somewhat of a surprise for them in their early forties. They'd tried after me, and after several miscarriages had given up, but then the big surprise. "And the best part of all," my mother would tell people, "is that after all those awful times, she was easy as pie." And if I was there, she'd look at me, tug on my chin, and say, "and a breeze compared to this one."

But then a year after Anna, it was the cancer, and she was gone. All that waiting and trying and giving up and then finally, something good, the girl she had always wanted. *What a gift she has left us,* the minister said at the funeral. Anna, the gift, was too little to be there. And when we got home later, after the cemetery and the ham sandwiches and cake at the church, I looked at Anna, and found myself wishing, just for a minute, that we could return the gift if it would mean bringing my mother back, and then I immediately felt terrible and picked up Anna, sitting quietly on the floor in the middle of relatives and neighbors playing with her colored blocks, and hugged her so hard she yelped like a puppy who'd been stepped on.

Before all that and way before Anna was born, there were the arguments about the farm—why things weren't working, what a mistake it had been. Early on, I'd figured out that you learn more by just watching and not asking questions, so I'd watch my mother and father huddle at the kitchen table, my mother hunched over her spiral notebook where she kept track of everything, calling out numbers to my father who punched them into a secondhand adding machine he got as a gift when he quit teaching to farm full-time. The other teachers who gave it to him joked that he'd need it to keep track of just how far in the hole he was going to go, not knowing how true that was going to be.

"How it's look?" my mother would ask.

My father shook his head.

"Well, how bad is it?"

"It's not good. Does the color red mean anything to you?"

"You're sure?"

"We've gone over it five times now. I can't change the numbers."

But they would go over it yet again, just to be sure, only to have it come out the same, if not worse.

And just to make things more complicated, it wasn't just any farm. It was my grandparents' place, and after they died, it went to my mother, their only child, who rented it out while she and my father lived in Minneapolis and she worked as a nurse while he taught junior high English. Eventually she talked him into giving dairy farming a try. He was tired of teaching and wanted to do something entirely different and more meaningful than teach eighth graders how to diagram sentences ("don't ask," he said when I asked him to explain how that worked), my mother told me. Something that was, well, closer to nature but still profitable. "I wanted your father to be the only farmer in Blue Earth County who could milk the cows and recite Shakespeare to them while he's doing it," my mother would respond when people asked why they gave up good, solid jobs to be tied down to a dairy farm, even though it had been her life until her parents died and she went to college. Then my father would add that if giving up the "learned life" of teaching was what it would take to make my mother happy, it was a small price.

At least that was the way I remembered them telling it; with my mother gone now, I don't hear that story very much anymore. And even when she was alive, there was the "public version"— the story of true love and taking risks and long days but making the world a healthy place with all the milk we were making—and the version with the notebook and the machine with the funny handle that my father would occasionally let me pull to add things up, and his frown when he saw the results.

Once, when I was five years old, I drew a picture of a cow and colored it green—my way of contributing to the cause while they were working on trying to make things balance out, even though they knew they wouldn't. I held it up to show them, but they were too busy having the Reggie Davidson argument again to pay attention to my masterpiece. It was the same argument that would come up again and again, when instead of artwork I would be working on long division, trying to keep an ear to the fight.

My father: "Ran into Reggie in town today."

My mother: "Let's not start that again."

"Corn's way, way up again. He's got his eye on another tractor."

My mother would try to ignore him and busy herself with the notebook. But my father wouldn't let it go. "I could have had it like *that.*" He'd snap his fingers. "But, nope. I'm stuck in a smelly barn morning, noon, and night up to my armpits in milk."

And my mother wouldn't let it go either. "Those cows are the reason you don't have to stand in front of a bunch of bored kids trying to get them to figure out how to use a comma properly. Is that what you want to go back to?"

When it got too loud, I'd wish for an older brother, a Wally, maybe, from old *Leave It To Beaver* reruns that were still on, or even one of those plastic-looking *Brady Bunch* boys with the long hair and striped T-shirts, someone I could talk to in the dark. *Did you hear that? What should we do? Do you think it's serious this time?* But all alone, I'd wrap my pillow around my head, hold it tight, and try to fall asleep.

My father pulls over, next to Reggie's field. "I know it's just going to irritate the hell out of me, but I have got to get a closer look."

"Can't we just go home? I have stuff to do." What was there to look at? When I was younger I'd go on rides with Grandpa Pete, my mother's father, to look at how things were doing in the county, even though the only fields he had were for the cows. Rows and rows of corn and soybeans, every plant and every field the same, separated only by fencing, going by forever out the window. If I wasn't bored, I was dizzy, and I went along only because he promised we'd stop for cones when we were done.

And what was the point of corn, really? Picked and then ground up and fed to hogs to make ham and bacon. There wasn't anything wrong with that—God knows we ate enough of those things—but in my mind it wasn't, well...noble, like what we did. Milk, cheese, and ice cream were just more... refined, not to mention the cows themselves. Living, breathing things, with faces, eyes, and personalities.

My father ignores me and gets out of the pickup. "Be right back."

"Dad, what are you doing?" I call after him. "We need to get home. Ellen's going to wonder what happened to us." Ellen runs a tight ship, and I picture her walking from the kitchen window to the front porch and then back again, worried that the pot roast and potatoes she makes three nights a week is going to dry out if we don't get a move on.

But there's more to it than just being a little late for supper. I wanted to get home to see if Andy Olnan had called, even though I know it's a long shot. We barely said two words to each other, and besides that he doesn't have our phone number (and, yes, we still have a landline). But if you really want to track somebody down in this town, it's not that difficult. We're the only Paulsens in the book, unless he got one of the s-o-n Paulsons but they'd just give him our number like they've done every other time someone was looking for us, the s-e-n Paulsens. A minor obstacle.

If you really want to track someone down. Of course that's the big question. And there I am, my insides about twenty years ahead of my brain. For all I know he could think I'm some loser guy, standing in line all by myself, that he happened to get stuck next to and he just had the good manners to be polite about it. But it can't hurt to hope, can it? Because I feel like I need to. Like it's the most important thing in the world.

"This'll just take a minute. I want to show you something. Something important."

He picks a row and starts walking, and then jogging, disappearing into Reggie Davidson's cornfield. Somebody from town might call it trespassing, but Reggie wouldn't have minded. In fact, he'd take it as a compliment. Even so, I scrunch down in my seat. If somebody else wanted to snoop around in Reggie's field, that was one thing, but there's no reason for people to know it's my father running through it like a crazy person.

When I sneak a look out the window a few minutes later, my father is ambling back through the corn, up the ditch to the pickup. He stops and lifts his face to the sun and smiles, acting like he's got nothing better to do than just enjoy the hot summer day. Bits of corn silk are stuck in his black hair, and he looks like he's wearing some sort of goofy yellow crown.

He gets into the pickup and holds up an ear of Reggie's corn that he's picked and peeled.

"What's that for?"

"Look at it. A goldmine. This is what we should be doing. *This.*" He waves the corn at me. "No more getting up at five every morning, no skipping vacations, no more playing nursemaid to sick calves, no more…" He starts the engine and pitches the ear of corn out his window, over the top of the pickup, back into Reggie Davidson's field. As he pulls onto the highway he catches a glimpse of himself in the rearview mirror, and the silk still in his hair. He plucks it out and throws that out the window too.

We're both quiet on the ride home, the only sound the scrunching of the pickup's tires on the gravel road. Maybe my father was right. You could be noble, as I liked to think we were, but what was so noble about being poor? And yet I don't think he wanted a future sitting on a tractor, planting, combining, and picking, day after day, year after year, any more than I did. But if not the cows, then what else was there for us?

And then there was my mother…the whole reason for this outing in the first place. Giving up, giving up on her. The lump in my throat is back now, and it stretches all the way to my stomach. We could either pull the plug now, or we could keep trying, even though we'd probably end up in the same place.

But I was leaving anyway, wasn't I? It'd be just a few more years for me, so did it make any difference to me what we did? My mother always said you can get through anything as long as you know it's going to end.

My mother. Taking her advice to get rid of something that was her life's work somehow isn't helping.

But for now, we'd still have the cows and the milking and things would have to stay the same. Making a change would take time, and nothing's going to happen today or tomorrow. Or the day after that. Chances are we'd get back into the routine and all of my father's business about quitting would be forgotten, at least for a while.

And until then, what else was there? School. Not my favorite thing but unless someone suddenly decided to home school me there wasn't much I could do about it. A means to an end: college and then who knows what.

And there was Andy Olnan, who was likely calling me at this very minute. I try to will my father to step on it, but he's ambling along, surveying the riches of someone's farm while trying to keep on eye on the road.

"What're you grinning about?" Apparently he's been watching me too.

"Nothing. I was just…thinking."

He doesn't ask me what about, and I'm glad. What would I have said? *I'm grinning because I'm thinking about a boy that I met for five minutes and now I'm in love?* And was that even really true? I don't know, but maybe. My father doesn't have a clue about what's going on with me, as far as I know. Or maybe he does and doesn't care or he has too many other things going on to worry about it or ask. We haven't yet had the "talk," the one where the two of us sit down after supper, and I give a big introduction along the lines of *I have something very, very important that I have to tell you,* and then boom! There it is. He looks shocked at first, but being a loving, liberal, educated, with-it sort of father he says, *That's okay, son, I still love you no matter what, it doesn't change anything,* all those things that the books tell parents to say.

Well, at least one book: *The Talk: What to Say (and Not Say) When Your Child Comes Out to You,* which I bought at the Barnes and Noble in Mankato while my father was shopping for some early Renaissance poetry or something and which I have hidden in the back of my sock drawer. I figured that it couldn't hurt to keep it on hand for him in case things didn't go that well when I told him.

To be honest, I've skimmed it more than I've actually read it, because I'm not really the target audience, but its step-by-step approach (step one: "listen and avoid the urge to overreact"; step two: "assure your child that you love him/her no matter what") should appeal to my father's sense of order, just as he likes supper and chores at the same time every day and reading formal poetry.

I know I'm making light of a very serious thing. And sooner or later, yes, I'll have to tell him, or he'll figure it out if he hasn't already. And if something happens with Andy Olnan, probably sooner.

But for now, he's a secret I want to keep all to myself, even though I know that makes me a secret too.

3

GREAT BOOTS

"Hey, Paulsen!"

I hear the snap of the towel, close my eyes, and wait for the sting. But this time Kent's only grazed the back of my thigh.

It's the Tuesday after Labor Day, the first hour of the first day of the start of the new school year, and another year of gym, another year with Kent Neustad. Thankfully it's my last one, but that only makes it all the worse, because I have a feeling that Kent is going to make sure it's a doozy.

"Shit," he says. "I'm losing my touch."

Towel snapping year after year as a form of harassment: yes, totally unoriginal (just like still requiring gym for everybody through sophomore year), but that pretty much describes Kent Neustad. Something that would require a little bit of planning and sophistication, like posting embarrassing pictures of someone on Facebook or Instagram…let's just say that's a little bit beyond Kent's capabilities. He's nothing if not consistent.

Kent should have been a senior, but because he'd repeated the first grade and then the fourth he was stuck in the tenth grade with the rest of us. To be held back once was bad enough, but twice had to have been some sort of record. But if Kent minded he didn't let on, because no matter what, he would always be two years ahead of everyone physically, if not academically. That was way more useful for intimidation.

Kent has had it in for me ever since we were in first grade Sunday school—my first and only time, his second. To avoid confusion his parents apparently thought it made sense for him to repeat Sunday school too. It started on the second Sunday of Advent, and we were working on construction paper figures for the manger scene. Kent had taken my Virgin Mary, made a spitball out of her, and launched her across the room. I retaliated by dumping a jar of glue on his head, a satisfying moment of revenge made even more so when Kent returned to class the next week with a shaved head, the only way his mother could deal with the sticky mess I'd made of his hair.

What followed from then on, every year, every class, was taunting (*Hey, Paulsen, are you a fairy or just a fag?*), tripping (*Hey, Paulsen, did you have a nice fall?* followed by Kent sticking out his leg and pushing me over it) and whatever other humiliations he could come up with. Regardless of his methods, it would always start the same way: *Hey, Paulsen!* I wasn't worthy of a whole name.

"That's enough, Zorro!" Mr. Todd, our gym teacher, yells from his office, just a few feet from the locker room, using the same nickname for Kent that he's used since seventh grade, never mind that none of us had a clue as to who Zorro was and what he had to do with towel snapping. Then he glares at me over his newspaper and shakes his head, as if Kent's obsession with splitting my backside open with red welts is somehow my fault.

As I peel off my T-shirt and shorts, already smelly from just one class, I think about the way gym was in elementary school, the simplicity of it. Back then there was no changing out of school clothes into gym clothes, then back into school clothes but only after taking the shower that Mr. Todd said that everyone, and he meant everyone, had to take, and no just running in and getting wet and running out again. The soap, the soap that the school provided for me, was there for a reason. And now, after running around the track three times, doing fifty push-ups, then around the track again followed by fifty more push-ups, the cool water and the mandatory soap does feel good, washing away the grime and the stickiness.

"Hey, Paulsen!" Kent takes the shower next to me, to keep me within range. There's somebody else using the shower on the other side of the room, but without my glasses I can't make him out. I shut my eyes tight and concentrate on getting some more lather going from the tiny bar of soap.

"Hey, Paulsen! Look at me! You can either look or plan on my fist meeting your fruity face when you least expect it."

That was a new one; usually Kent's threats weren't quite that original. It must have taken him most of the summer to put that one together. But a threat is a threat, and since there was always the possibility he might actually follow through, I turn around and open my eyes. Kent pivots his hips forward and backward, making his penis flop up and down, then finishes the little dance with a big thrust of his groin my direction.

"Take a good look, Paulsen," he hisses. "I always knew you were a fucking fag."

I shut my eyes again and scrub my face under the rushing water, like I'm trying to wash away what he'd said, even though I'd long ago talked myself into believing that his taunts didn't hurt me anymore. But of course that wasn't true. Each time was still like the first time, many years ago, when I complained to my mother about what he'd called me without really knowing what it meant, and she winced and had to look away. But then she reached out and held my face and told me that it was Kent's problem, not mine, and there were people in the world who wanted nothing more than to hurt you, and there always would be, and you had to just…And then she trailed off, not sure what advice to give. You had to…be better than they were, she finally said, though she couldn't say exactly how I would do that. And from then on, every time Kent went after me, I told her about it, until I stopped because there was still no answer.

And just to make it worse, there's no getting around the fact that Kent has grown from a skinny and delicate boy into a good-looking young man, with curly brown hair, blue eyes, perfect skin, thick upper arms and chest. And being two years older than everybody else, he's also considerably more, well, *developed* than the rest of us, and he made sure everyone knew that, especially me. Even boys who weren't attracted to boys, and never would be, can't help looking at him, if for no other reason than to hope that, maybe in a short couple of years, they might all look like that too. So where does that put me? On the one hand, I want to look at him at every possible opportunity, but I also don't want to be covered in towel snap-induced welts. It's a dilemma when your body tells you one thing and your mind something else.

After two leisurely rounds of shampooing my hair to buy some time, finally I hear the clomp-clomp of Kent's big feet slapping against the wet floor, out into the locker room. All clear.

"What an asshole. You shouldn't let him talk to you like that."

It takes me a moment to recognize him now, his blond hair now darker from the water, almost covering his eyes.

It's another stare down with Andy Olnan, though this time we're both wet and naked, and once again I try to think of something to say and once again nothing will come.

"Thanks…I mean, I know." Even under the hot water I'm shaking a little bit. "He really is an—"

"Asshole. You can say it. It's okay."

"Asshole."

"Now you got it." He smiles at me, turns off the water, and starts toward the locker room. Then he stops and turns around. "You coming?"

"Um, yup."

Yup. It sounds like something my father would say, talking to the guy at the feed store, shooting the breeze. Ugh. But at least it's something.

At my locker, I dry off quickly while keeping an eye out for Andy Olnan, who must be changing in another part of the room. I need to get dressed and then catch him so I can demonstrate that I really can do more than just stare with my mouth open and that I do have more intelligent things to say other than "yup." How many more chances will I get?

I try to stick my key into the lock, but somebody's just-chewed Juicy Fruit is jammed up in there. Nice. I work on digging it out while also trying not to gag, but it's a stringy, wet, disgusting mess, and it's stuck so far in there I'll never get all of it out. Now what? I look around for Mr. Todd who, as usual, has disappeared, though I doubt there'd be much he'd do anyway, other than make it my fault too.

"Something wrong, Paulsen?" Kent walks toward me, tucking in his shirt. "You better hurry up. You don't want to be late for class. Not Perfect Paulsen." He yanks on the towel around my waist and it falls to the floor.

"PP. That's a great name for you." He chuckles. "Faggot PP with the small PP." He picks up my towel and snaps it at me, three, four, five times, sending me into a crazy dance as I try to guard my crotch because, of all the places, the sting there would be the worst of all.

Andy Olnan, fully dressed, his hair neatly combed, puts his index finger up to his lips, tiptoes behind Kent, grabs the towel out of his hands and tosses it to me. "Real smart, Neustad."

Kent glares at him. "Who the hell are you? And how do you even know my name?"

"When someone's a dickhead, word gets around." Andy Olnan motions for me to get out of the way. He takes a deep breath, and with one kick of a cowboy boot, my locker's open, the handle clattering across the floor.

"Jeez," Kent says. He puts up his hands, mumbles something about getting to class, and slinks away.

"You better hurry. We gotta get out of here before Todd finds out I trashed your locker."

"God, I hate that Kent Neustad," I say, pulling on my jeans and shirt.

"Me too. And I just met him."

"Believe me, you haven't missed anything. I know."

"I sort of figured that." He smiles at me.

"I hope you don't get in trouble. Because of me."

He shrugs. "It wouldn't be the first time."

"And I hope nothing happened to your cowboy boots. Boot, I mean. It's—I mean they—are pretty nice." *Pretty nice.* I should just shoot myself.

"Thanks." He lifts the boot up, inspecting for damage. "Looks okay to me."

"I'm glad."

And when I have everything on and my shoes are tied, we're off, running through the halls together, working up yet another sweat.

The rest of the day passes mercifully fast, even with the usual first day blah, blah, blah lectures six times over about papers, tests, homework. Then it's supper and the usual *how was your first day* questions (fine, fine, fine) and then chores, and then finally I'm in bed, where I can go over the day again and again: Andy Olnan in the shower, tossing his hair back to get the water out; Andy Olnan saving me from Kent Neustad with his cowboy boots that I thought were sort of lame at first; Andy Olnan smiling at me; Andy Olnan following me around almost the whole day, next to me, hanging on to my every word about our school, about this teacher and that one, who's in and who's out in our class…well, maybe not *hanging,* but listening. Someone was listening, paying attention. To me.

And it's only the first day.

I'm too wound up to sleep, so I do what I always do when I have insomnia: I look at my ancient Sears catalog which used to belong to my Grandma Davidson, and then to my mother, and now it's mine. Anybody else would be playing games on their laptop or phone, but I don't have a computer for pretty much the same reasons that I don't have a cell phone: my father and his whole anti-technology crusade. What little online time I had was limited to whatever I could squeeze in at school on the school computers, usually looking something up for an assignment. Everyone else was on social media, but without a computer of my own, what was the point? Not only that, but the minute you hopped on to Instagram or whatever, one of the librarians was sure to be breathing down your neck, reminding you that the computers were for "schoolwork related" purposes. And as far as my father was concerned, the computer, along with its evil stepsibling the cell phone, was equally responsible for the decline of American, if not world, civilization. If I needed to write something, the old IBM Selectric typewriter that my mother used for the farm business stuff was more than adequate. And maybe even better, my father said, because I'd have to think hard about what I was going to say and I couldn't rely on fancy cutting and pasting to do it for me. *It builds character,* he'd say, when I asked why I couldn't even have a secondhand computer. That was often his go-to answer to pretty much everything, whether it was why he got out of teaching and into farming, and even my mother dying. *I know how hard this is, but there are things in life that test us and build character and make us stronger.* I wanted to tell him that I'd rather have less character if it meant keeping my mother instead, but I knew he meant well.

Still, even if I had the computer and the phone, I'd still keep up my catalog routine. My mother loved old catalogs and could spend hours with them, poring over the clothes, the sheets and towels, pots and pans, even though she couldn't buy them any-more, but sometimes she just liked to look and make comments about the models. "My God! Look at her. She's so skinny she's about to dry up and blow away!" After long days of chores and cooking, she was happiest when she had nothing to do but sit on the couch, with Anna and a catalog on her lap, and me next to her. And later, when she was in the hospital, the one thing she wanted more than anything else was her catalog. "Better than the Bible itself," she said when I brought it to her. When I asked why, she said, "Because it gives me comfort, and when I look at it I feel like I'm on the couch again, in my own house, instead of in this bed."

So of course keeping one of her catalogs is a way to re-member her, but there's another reason. There's a picture of a man in it. He has a very square jaw, which he holds between his thumb and index finger like he's thinking about something very important. He has black hair and long side burns (which were apparently big back then), perfect white teeth, and a perfectly proportioned body: not too big, but not too skinny. It's well, perfect, like everything else about him. To me he's a cross be-tween one of the Greek sculptures we looked at in art class and Superman, if he ever decided to model underwear.

When I was eleven I looked up *homosexual* in the dictionary:

sexual desire toward another of the same sex. Was it the man in the catalog that led me to find the word, or was it something else? But it wasn't a big mystery. I wasn't afraid. But how did I even know to look *homosexual* up in the first place? I can't remember, exactly, but I must have heard the word from somewhere. Kent Neustad, maybe? Doubtful. Too big a word for him. Television? We had one, but we didn't watch it very much, and we still don't. A huge time waster, Mom and Dad said, though it was good to have for the weather.

I did read the newspaper. Now that was something my parents believed in, because it was how I learned to read in the first place. Rather than sitting on my mother or father's lap with a picture book, we'd have the newspaper open in front of us, and they'd point to little words in the big headlines. My father now does the same thing with Anna. *It never hurts to start early,* he says. *We did the same thing with you, and look how brilliant you are!* I hoped he was serious.

After my dictionary discovery, for a while, whenever I discovered mention of the word *homosexual* in a newspaper or journal I would tear it out and put it between the pages of the dictionary. Somewhere along the line, though I don't remember exactly when, I started looking for articles that mentioned *gay* in them, because I understood it was the same thing. Nobody told me; somehow I figured it out. The last article I kept was about something that had happened in Minneapolis: a bunch of men in a car pulled over and started beating up some other men standing outside a gay bar, calling them derogatory names while they were doing it. The article didn't mention what those names were, but I had a hunch they were same names Kent Neustad had been calling me for a long time now.

If that could happen in Minneapolis, where I might want to be someday, because there you could be whoever you wanted to be, what did it say about Fullerton? Maybe Kent Neustad was the least of my problems, and a lot of people around me thought like him. He was just saying it out loud.

What was it my father liked to say? *The more things change, the more they stay the same.*

But what other choice did I have? This was it. This was me. I'd have to not be afraid, or at least pretend that I wasn't.

Maybe someday I'd have my "another"—the another from the dictionary. If you had someone else, you'd be less afraid, wouldn't you? But for now, though the only "another" I had was catalog guy, who would always be there, frozen forever, standing around in his underwear.

I rub the shiny paper with my fingers now and pretend it's his skin I'm touching, his hair. I try to imagine, like I always do, but for the first time, I don't feel anything, except embarrassed and a little sad because he's all I have.

But maybe it also means I'm ready for something real.

Maybe Andy Olnan could be my another. A living, breathing one.

It's something I want to find out.

4

ALPHABETICAL ORDER

When I get to school now, Andy Olnan is there, waiting at my locker, like it was the most perfectly logical and natural thing to happen. I say hi, he says hi, and that's all there is to it. We walk to our first class together, then meet up after and walk to the next one.

It took forever, or maybe it just seemed like it, but I'm finally hanging out with someone. Me, who'd never been much of a hanger outer.

Or maybe it was just me following him around, or maybe he was following me around. It was like when we first met. When we touched, who let go first? Or when we first looked at each other, who stared the longest?

But did it even matter?

Because it feels like something is happening, even if we didn't talk about what it was, which would of course have been entirely too weird, or to put into words that I heard a lot, too *gay* (even when the particular thing had absolutely nothing to do with being gay), though maybe this actually did for once.

We sit together at lunch every day that first week. Before that it wasn't like I ate all by myself—I wasn't that big of a loser—but I usually sat at the end with some of the boys, boys I'd known as long as I'd known Kent Neustad, who let me join them but expected nothing from me in terms of conversation, and vice versa. We had…an *understanding*, I guess. But sometimes when I sat down at my usual place there was often a whisper, and sometimes then a laugh, and I knew it was something about me. Some things you just know. Was that better than sitting alone? I guess it must have been, because I kept on doing it.

But then I showed up with Andy, and for the first time ever

there was actually someone sitting across from me, rather than an empty space. I didn't have to lean in to make it seem like I was part of the conversation. Andy and I had our own, and maybe I had my *another.*

That first day the other boys mostly just grunted and nodded at Andy, in the way that boys do because it would not be cool to look too interested. But Andy had manners. He went around, shook hands, just like he'd done with me, asking them their names, as polite as could be. Then we went back to our end of the table, and it was just him and me, which made me happy. I wanted him all to myself.

But that wasn't completely true. So after a week's gone by and it's looking more and more likely that Andy Olnan might actually be viable (as a friend, at least), I casually mention him at supper. It was important to me that my father, and for Ellen too, to know that, all appearances aside, I wasn't a complete outcast. And what if Andy turned into something more? It certainly couldn't hurt to lay the groundwork now.

While my father doesn't say *a friend? You? There's hope after all!* I can tell he's pleased. "Well, that's good. You'll have to invite him for supper. What did you say his last name was?"

"Olnan. O-L-N—"

My father interrupts me. "Well, what do you know. Must be Spud Olnan's boy."

"*Spud?* What kind of name is that?" I ask him.

"That's what we called him back in high school. We were in the same class."

"He just moved here. From Minneapolis," I say. "Andy, I mean."

"So the rumor turned out to be true," my father says.

"What rumor?" Ellen asks, passing me the corn.

"That they were moving back down here to take over the old Jensen place."

"Who's they?" Andy and I hadn't gotten too far into our family histories yet, so I hadn't given much thought to who he might belong to, or why he even ended up here, other than that he was living on a farm, like me. I was just glad that he had, and

I didn't care about the rest. We'd get to it eventually, wouldn't we?

"I assume Spud and his wife had kids," my father says. "One of whom must be your new friend. What's his name again?"

"Andy." I like saying his name, so I say it again. "It's Andy."

"Well, Ida Jensen is his grandmother, on his mother's side."

The first thing that comes into my head: *He was probably here visiting, more than once, and I didn't even know it. Just a mile away!*

"How come you called him Spud?" Ellen asks.

My father smiles. "He tended to be a bit on the pudgy side. All the way back to grade school. I don't think he minded it all that much."

Ellen laughs, but I wonder how my father knew that. It wasn't the most flattering nickname you could call a person. "So are they going to farm?"

"I imagine so. Though I thought Spud was doing pretty well up in the Cities. Had his own high-tech company making something or other. Doesn't make any sense why he'd give that up and come back here to try to farm. Usually it's the other way around." My father gives me a look. "And heck, I don't think Marge Olnan has set foot on the place since her mother died five years ago. I also heard she'd gotten involved in some sort of fringe religious group."

"Like a cult?" I ask. Andy had just gotten even more interesting.

"I don't think I'd go that far. But when she'd come back to town for a visit, when her mother was still alive, you'd run into her in town and every other word was praise the Lord this and praise the Lord that." He laughs and shakes his head, like he's remembering something. "Used to drive your mother absolutely around the bend. Spud was never like that, but who knows what gets into people? And coming back to farm with not a clue about what you're doing just because someone hands it to you? What are they thinking?"

"But aren't they sort of like us? I mean, we got the farm from Grandma and Grandpa Davidson. Well, Mom did and she sort of gave it to you, didn't she?"

My father raises his eyebrows but doesn't say anything.

"The only difference is that we're dairy. Otherwise it's kind of the same thing. Isn't it?"

"I'm not sure that it is," my father says, lightly, though I can tell he's annoyed by the way he digs into his mashed potatoes. "All I can say is, good luck! He's going to need it."

And besides, you didn't know "diddlysquat" about dairy farming. I only think the last part. Better not take this too far.

And what did it matter how or why they ended up here or whether they know what to do? They'd figure it out, just like we did. And maybe they'd be better at it, though that would be sure to drive my father crazy. And in the end, no matter what he said, we're not going to go anywhere.

But the very best part of it: if it hadn't been for Ida Jensen, I never would have met Andy Olnan.

Thanks, Grandma Jensen.

A few days later, because it's beautiful outside, Andy Olnan and I ditch the usual guy table, wrap up our lunch in some napkins, and sit outside on the grass for some fresh air. The only problem is that, because of the direction of the wind, the smell of manure is so strong that we may as well be out in the middle of a soybean field. It doesn't bother me—I'm used to it—but Andy is another story.

"God almighty, that stench. You'd think we'd be safe here in town, but nope, it's everywhere. I feel like I need to wash my hair ten times a day and it still stinks."

"You'll get used to it," I say. "Before long you won't even notice it. You know…" I'd been rehearsing my next line since last night, after hearing the story about his grandmother and their farm. "You know, we…have something in common. You and me." *There. Why was that so hard?*

"Really? Besides us both being stuck in this school with those Neanderthals we've been sitting with in the lunch room?"

"What do you mean?" Even though I think I have a pretty good idea what he means. We're not like them, Andy Olnan and me. We're…apart. Special. A group of our own. I feel like I could float away.

"Well, they're okay, I guess. I just don't find them all that stimulating to talk to. At least not for very long. Know what I mean?"

"I think I do." Does that mean Andy Olnan finds *me* stimulating? He didn't say that, exactly, but I'm going with it. I take a bite of my Sloppy Joe, which despite being as greasy and oversalted as always, never tasted better.

"I had a feeling you would." Andy Olnan smiles. "What were you saying about a thing we had in common? I sort of went off."

I tell him about last night's supper conversation with my father though I of course leave out the "diddlysquat" part and I don't refer to Andy's dad as "Spud." Despite what my father said, maybe the Olnans are sensitive about it, so why take the risk? "Funny, isn't it? What a coincidence."

"Yeah, I suppose." He smiles again, though this time it's one of those forced smiles people give you when they're just going along to be nice.

"I just thought it was…interesting that each of us is living on our grandparents' farms." *Interesting.* Could I be any more smooth? Ugh.

"Yeah, I suppose." He combs his hair with his fingers. That hair again. "Yeah, good old Grandma Ida. God bless her for leaving us the place. How *convenient.*" He says it with a bit of a sneer.

"Convenient? How so?"

Andy looks past me, like he's gone somewhere else. "Nothing. I'll tell you about it sometime. Maybe." He laughs softly. "So your grandma gave you a farm too."

"Well, to my mom, really. She already had it when she married my dad. She liked it a lot. She and my dad were really into it. But now my dad is sort of…" I stop. Now *I'm* the one going somewhere else. Somewhere I really don't want to go.

"Liked? As in she doesn't like it anymore?"

"She died a couple of years ago." The words stick in my throat a bit. It's weird, but it's the first time I've ever told anyone. In this town you really don't have to, because everybody knows already.

"Oh man. That must be rough." I wish he would touch me, even if it's just a totally hetero shoulder squeeze or something, but I feel guilty for wanting it at the same time we're talking about my mother. "I'm not crazy about my mom and I give her a hard time sometimes, but it would be a bummer if she wasn't around. What did she die of?"

"Cancer." Again, it's like I'm speaking a foreign language. Had I ever said the word to anyone out loud before? Probably not, though my father had said it plenty of times when he had to tell me what was going on with my mother: *It's breast cancer... they hope they got it early, but we don't know...the cancer's spread... chemo only works for so long on cancer, and then we'll need to explore other options.* The cancer this, the cancer that. After a while, if I heard the word one more time, I thought I'd go off the deep end. As if he knew or because he was tired of the word too, my father started referring to as an "it": *it's in her lungs now...it's gotten bigger...once it's spread there, it's tough to do much more.*

"Oh man," Andy says again. "My grandpa had that. He smoked like a chimney, and by the time they found it, too late."

"I know," I say, though my mother was the healthiest person in the world, never smoked, drank hardly at all, even thought about us going vegetarian until my father said there was no way that was going to happen. But at least he's trying to relate. "So what are you going to do on your farm?" Time to change the subject. "Dairy, crops, hogs?"

Andy Olnan frowns. "What do you mean?"

"What kind of farming are you going to do?"

"Hell if I know. It's a farm. I was brought here against my will. I don't plan on getting involved."

"What about chores?"

"Chores? Unless I missed something, slavery's supposed to be against the Constitution."

I don't know what to make of that. If you were a kid and

you lived on a farm, you did chores. End of story. I was hooking up milking machines when I was six and helped my mother deliver a calf not long after that. "So what are you going to do?" "Like I said, as little as possible. I'm a city boy, remember? My old man can't make me do anything I don't want to do. Having to live out there under lock and key in the middle of nowhere is enough punishment. That plus the wacko church my mom says we have to join." He takes a swig of his milk and slams the carton down hard, so that a little bit spills over the side on to the grass.

"What wacko church?" Maybe my father had been right after all.

He combs his hair again with his fingers, this time pulling on it more. "I really don't want to get into it."

Brought here against my will. Punishment. Lock and key. Like he's some sort of POW or something. Though really, wasn't that true for any kid? What choice did any of us have about anything, when you really thought about it? But for Andy Olnan, it was different, somehow worse, at least to hear him tell it. I imagine telling my father that nope, no more chores for me, you can't make me, I'm on strike…and I laugh out loud.

"What's so funny?"

"Nothing. I was just thinking about chores, and telling my dad I don't want to do them anymore. He'd go into orbit."

"Well, you're a person," Andy says. "You have rights."

"Maybe. But it's…sort of like a business for us, isn't it?" I ask it like I'm not sure, even though I of course know better. And ours isn't doing so hot at the moment. Probably not the best time to try to bail, even if I could.

But Andy Olnan's not having it. "Business," he snorts. "Maybe for you. If it is, I'll take my money up front. No more farms, no more church."

What money? And what church? I want to ask, but then the bell rings.

"Back to prison." Andy sighs and tilts his head in the direct of the school building. "If you're not in one kind, you're in another."

Believe it or not, the whole time I've been in school, Charles Osterman is the first male teacher I've ever had, and with his white mustache and long, full beard, and his round belly, big as a basketball hanging over his belt, he looks like he'd make a better Santa than an earth science teacher. It's the first day of lab, and after some endless and mind-numbing lectures along with required tedious note taking, we're finally getting around to doing some actual experiments. "You'll just have to wait," he'd said when someone dared to ask the first day of class when we'd actually get to look at some real rocks, up close. "You can't dance until you know the steps."

Everyone had groaned then. Now, there's at least a little bit of excitement in the room, even though we're all sleepy from lunch, because he'll eventually have to stop talking and let us *do* something before the end of the hour, as he promised. But not before he explains what he calls our "LPRs" (Laboratory Procedure Reports) and how we are supposed to complete them down to the last ridiculous detail: where our names go (top left, not top right); all "paper dandruff" (the little specks that come from tearing the page out of a spiral notebook) must be removed; papers written in pencil are strictly forbidden. Any papers violating the rules will be returned to the owner with a "big fat goose egg," and when it's clear that none of us know what he's talking about, he walks over the blackboard and draws a zero that takes up an entire section. On and on he goes.

I watch Andy Olnan, sitting two people over from me, and the way he leans back in his chair, his eyes half-closed and his arms folded casually behind his head, looking like he might start whistling at any moment. And yet somehow he knows when to sit up straight, feet on the floor, eyes on the board because Mr. Osterman is about to look at him.

But before long I realize that Mr. Osterman is watching me watching Andy, even as he drones on and on. If he eventually locks eyes with one of us, he'll have an excuse to stop everything and say something about how he would appreciate everyone's undivided attention, his way of shutting us down without necessarily embarrassing us. And if that doesn't work, he'll go to the next level (calling us out by name), and if that fails, then an invitation to visit the principal's office. My father is right. Teachers needed to be able to have five sets of eyes to do the job, one of the reasons he got out, he said. *If I wanted to be a cop, I'd have become one.*

To keep both of us from getting into trouble, I put my head down and pretend to take notes, like I'm trying to get every last word Mr. Osterman says down because they're all very important. But instead of notes I'm drawing a portrait of Andy Olnan. I'm no artist, but I think I'm getting the shape of his face, how his chin and cheekbones are sharp, almost pointy, his thick fingers now tucked halfway into his front pockets. But his hair, my favorite thing, is another story; it looks more like spaghetti than anything else. And the eyes aren't the best either—too squinty, like he's trying to read something but needs glasses to do it. Not the least bit cool. But overall, not too bad.

When I look up from my work, Mr. Osterman is right in front of me, looking down, still talking about granite and sediment and layers and who knows what else. I slide the paper under my notebook, take out another sheet, and start taking notes—this time for real.

"Ladies and gentleman, there is one other important aspect of good laboratory practice that merits consideration." He starts talking about how we'll be working in pairs during lab sessions. Finally something worth paying attention to. He says he will be assigning partners alphabetically, which naturally means that, with the whole "O" and "P" situation, Andy and I have a pretty decent chance of being together.

"You will do everything equally, operating as one." Mr. Osterman holds up his two index fingers far apart, then slowly brings them closer and closer until they're touching. "Got it?"

Everyone nods, except Andy. As soon as Mr. Osterman turns to write something on the board, Andy sticks one of his index fingers up his nose, looks at me, and then looks around the room to make sure everyone has seen it too. Then everyone is laughing, even Kent Neustad, who gives Andy a thumbs-up.

By the time Mr. Osterman turns around Andy's finger is safely out of his nose, his hands folded innocently in his lap. "Mr. Olnan? Is there something you find funny here? Maybe you could let us all in on it." As much I hate to admit it, my father is right. Teachers really do have eyes everywhere.

"Um, no, it's just that…" Andy can't stop giggling. "What are we supposed to do with our fingers?" Everyone is laughing again, and I'm laughing too, and not just my usual laugh that is more like a smile and two or three quiet chuckles to make it look like you're trying to be a good sport. For the first time in my life, and because it's Andy, I'm one of the loud ones.

"Mr. Paulsen?"

I stop laughing. I'm not sure how I'm supposed to reply, in the new world of tenth grade, where you can be a mister. *Yes, sir?* So instead I sit there, staring, my face burning.

"I'm just thinking now of the long, long semester ahead that you are likely to have with Mr. Olnan as your partner. My sympathies."

Everyone laughs again and looks at Andy, which means I can too. He smiles at me, and I can breathe again.

"So. Where were we? Oh, right, lab partners." Mr. Osterman starts writing names on the board, putting them together in pairs. *Olnan and Thompson. Martin and Paulsen.*

So much for Olnan and Paulsen, the dynamic duo who were going to take earth science class, if not the entire school, by storm. But I look straight ahead at my name not next to Andy's and nod, as if this was the plan along and I'm totally fine with it. On with the rocks!

As we all get up and shuffle off to meet with our new partners, I take another look at Andy's portrait. I'd planned to show it to him when we started looking at rocks together, but his left eyebrow's unfinished, his smile is crooked, his hair…yes, perfect spaghetti. Not so good after all.

I've known Cathy Martin for as long as I've known Kent Neustad. She was an eyewitness to the Virgin Mary beheading in Sunday school, and my guess is that she, like pretty much everyone else in the class, wanted to dump that glue on him as much as I did. She'd put up with a lot of Kent's harassment, too, in her case being called a "bra" whenever he saw her. She'd blush, just like I did when Kent took aim at me. Besides our mutual hatred (and fear) of Kent Neustad, we had other things in common as well. The Martins are dairy farmers, too, just down the road from us, though on a much larger scale: forty cows, twice what we have, plus hogs and a couple of cornfields. But according to my father, the rumor was that Chip Martin, Cathy's father, was in over his head with the bank because he was trying to do too much. But even if it was just talk, that didn't prevent my father from offering some advice, even though Chip didn't ask for it: "You should sell every last one of those cows, just like we should sell ours. If every dairy farmer in this county did that, we'd all be a lot better off." How or why that would help, he didn't say, and I didn't ask. It was just more talk, because no matter what he said we'd never get out of dairy farming any more than we'd suddenly start growing coconuts.

If things are bad at home, Cathy doesn't let on. She's perfectly behaved and perfectly groomed at all times, her thick blond hair usually pulled back into a tight ponytail, nothing ever out of place. She's pretty, I guess, though to be honest I haven't paid that much attention. She has always been the best student all through school, in every class and in every subject. She'll no doubt be the high school valedictorian two years from now and head off to Carleton or Saint Olaf College in Northfield, not that far away but where all the valedictorians from Fullerton High usually go, or maybe even somewhere out east. She's so smart that she'll probably get a free ride, so it wouldn't matter if her parents went broke or not.

"I'm really sorry," Cathy whispers to me. We're supposed to be looking at some rocks that Mr. Osterman has given us and then answer a bunch of questions: *Look carefully at your specimen. Identify the striations you see, noting color and texture.* She picks up our rock, turns it over a few times, and starts jotting notes in her notebook.

"Sorry for what?" I whisper back.

"That you didn't get to be with Andy. I know you wanted to be."

This is typical Cathy: always saying the right thing, apologizing for something that wasn't even her fault. The first day I was back at school after my mother died, she came to my locker to tell me how sorry she was. Other than teachers, she was the only person to say anything to me about it. To be fair, I wouldn't have known what to say to me either. But even before that she had kept up on my mother's treatment, asking how she was getting along, if there was anything she or her family could do, even though they'd already been sending over cakes and casseroles during the entire time my mother had been sick.

"It's okay," I say. It's the same answer I'd given before when we'd talked about my mother. Not *thank you*, or *I really appreciate that*, or something that was more from the heart. Having just lost my mother, it wasn't okay, of course, and it embarrassed me to think that I'd answered like that, that I hadn't acted more… sorry, even though it was something beyond sorry, something that I didn't know how to say, and maybe never would.

Instead of working with Cathy on our rocks, like I'm supposed to be doing, I watch Andy Olnan with Dave Thompson, who's good at sports but not much else, the two of them playing catch with one of their rocks until Mr. Osterman tells them they can either get down to business immediately or enjoy the pleasure of his company at detention after school. Andy looks back at me, shrugs his shoulders, and smiles.

Cathy and I work quietly for the rest of the period, keeping the chitchat to a minimum, and I try not to look at Andy anymore. When we're finished, we hand in our LPR to Mr. Osterman, who grades it at his desk while we wait: *100 points,* he writes at the top, and underneath that, *Excellent* and GREAT TEAMWORK! underlined three times.

"You really lucked out," Andy says. We're on the bus ride home, and he's just replayed his comedy act in earth science. Except for just a few people in the back who are either on their phones or listening to music, we're the only ones left. "The only rocks

Dave Thompson knows about are the ones in his head." Andy laughs at his joke, but I don't. "We got a whopping 75 on our report. Let me guess what you guys got. A 95?"

"100." Even though I should be thrilled, it comes out sounding like I'm embarrassed.

"Figures. But Cathy's not bad. Sometime, when she's leaning over the microscope, you should get close and lean over too, and then cop a feel, and pretend like it was an accident."

"But if I actually did it, how would I make it seem like an accident? Wouldn't she know I was doing it?" I can't help being logical, even when it comes to something I know nothing about—girls. And in the end it doesn't matter, because I wouldn't want to do it in the first place. I'm not interested in feeling up Cathy Williams or any other girl.

But maybe Andy Olnan is. How is it possible that the thought never crossed my mind?

"What's wrong? You seem a little pissed off or something."

I take a deep breath and think about what I'm going to say. "I was just counting on… I mean, I thought we were going to be partners. And now we're not."

Andy looks out the window. "Jeez. What's the big deal? She's a lot smarter than me anyway."

For the rest of the way home, we're both quiet. I wonder if we've just had our first fight, and if I've already blown it with Andy Olnan. Instead, we look out the window at the fields, at the corn that will be ready to be picked in just a few weeks, at the cows eating the grass, still green but that won't be for much longer.

Andy's stop is before mine. "See you tomorrow," he says as he makes his way to the door. "More good times with Mr. Osterman, right?" When he gets to the bottom step he turns and smiles at me, and as the door closes, he waves.

I spend the rest of the ride thinking about what it would be like to go off the deep end for someone, especially someone who may not even be interested in another boy, and I realize I already have.

"So? Do you feel any smarter?" Ellen asks. She and Anna are at the kitchen sink, Anna standing on a chair, giving Anna's favorite doll, Cindy, a bath. Anna has one of my mother's old aprons tied around her neck like a bib to keep her from getting wet. It has a red-and-white-checkered pattern, and while I recognize it I can't remember ever seeing my mother wearing it. Did she even wear aprons? What *did* she wear? Not remembering something about her worries me, but I'm not sure what to do about it. The harder I try to remember the less I remember, so I try hard all over again, and it becomes…what? A vicious cycle, I guess. And if I don't try, doesn't that make me a bad son? There's no winning.

"Not yet." I take two peanut butter cookies from the Tupperware box on the counter.

"That's okay. You've got a few years for it all to sink in." Ellen puts Anna down and gives her a cookie, which she offers to Cindy before taking a bite.

"It…was sort of a weird day."

"How so?"

"It's too complicated to explain." Where would I even start? *I sort of like this boy but I don't think he likes me, or "likes" me in that way, and oh by the way did I ever tell you I like boys?*

"Suit yourself. You'd better get going on chores. You're on your own because your dad had to run an errand in Mankato."

When my father first brought up the idea of having someone live with us after my mother died I hadn't really seen the point, at least as it affected me. I didn't need a babysitter, but we did someone to look after Anna. My father and I couldn't do the milking, watch her, cook, and take care of the house all at the same time. Anna needed a mother, even if we had to hire one for her. As for me, I'd already had a mother. I didn't want another one.

At first I couldn't understand why an eighteen-year-old girl wouldn't be getting out of Fullerton the first chance she got, much less why she'd want to live with *us*, even if she was getting paid for it. Later on, after the decision was made and my father had brought her over with her things, he explained that the

Hansens were selling their farm and moving to town and she didn't want to be far away from them, not after her father's accident a year earlier, especially since she was their only child. He'd gotten too close to the power takeoff on a corn picker, his pants leg got caught, and the next thing he knew his leg was gone. "Just like that," my father said, before he launched into a lecture about how on a farm you had to be on guard all the time for accidents, *let that be a lesson,* even though the only machinery we used were the milking machines, which seemed harmless. And the cows, too, so long as you stayed alert and gave them their space to avoid getting kicked (something I knew from age three).

Now that she has been with us for a while, it seems like she's always been here, and Anna loves her, which is the most important thing. As for me, we get along fine, though it's not like she's become the older sister I never had, never mind a mother substitute. The only mother I needed was gone. We never have had a deep life conversation, even though I suppose we could; she's only a few years older than me, though she seems a lot older. *Girls mature a lot faster than boys,* my mother once told me. Or maybe it's more about what she's gone through: having to watch her father deal with a terrible accident and give up farming, and then moving in with a strange family so you can earn a living. But mostly she and I talk about everyday things, like *I'm washing clothes today, so be sure to throw your dirty stuff in the hamper,* though at first even that wasn't such an everyday thing. Even after she moved in I was still doing my own laundry, until my father told me not to because that made her feel bad, like she wasn't doing her job, and that was the whole point of having her here in the first place. I told him that I didn't mind, even though the truth was I felt embarrassed having her touch my clothes, especially my underwear. Some things were just too private.

But if I were to be perfectly honest, I was really worried that, if I was okay with her washing my underwear, what would happen next? Would she go even further down the mother path with me? And how would I respond? I wouldn't want to be rude, but like I said, I've had a mother, and I don't want a replacement.

But after a while, it really didn't matter. She really did just want to do the laundry—all of it—because that was her job, as was cooking, cleaning, helping with chores now and then, and most of all taking care of Anna.

That was a relief, but at the same time I wondered if, even if she didn't mother me, she still might be someone I could tell things to: someone older, not as old as a parent, but old enough to give me advice. About what, I didn't know, but it might be nice if the option was there. But Ellen was all business. No heart to hearts, deep life conversations, or whatever you wanted to call them, were in my future anytime soon.

Up in my room I finish my cookies, get out of my school clothes and into my chore clothes, and wonder what choreless Andy Olnan must be doing at this very moment: playing video games, maybe, or watching television, probably eating potato chips and drinking a Mountain Dew, while I'm trudging out to the barn to do the same thing I've done almost every day for practically my whole life. Maybe my father is right. Let's just sell off the whole herd, plant corn or soy beans like everybody else is doing and start over. Or sell everything, buy a nice new house in town with good plumbing and a finished basement. He could go back to teaching, meet a nice single teacher and get married again so Anna could have a real mother. And I wouldn't smell like sour milk and manure anymore.

Some of the cows are already by the barn door, while the others are farther out in the pasture, waiting for the signal that it's time. It's always the same ones who want to be first and the same ones who like to be coaxed. Cows like order, predictability, structure…like people. My father saw that in one of the farm magazines that he used to subscribe to when he and my mother first started farming together. She laughed when he read that to her one night after supper. "I could have told you that," she said. "Typical teacher. Needs to have everything in writing."

She was teasing him, but it was the truth. My father wanted certainty as much as the cows did. No wonder he's thinking about getting out.

I take the rusty bell off the wall, the bell that belonged to my grandfather who started the farm, and swing it back and forth exactly fifteen times. Within a few minutes the cows are all lined up, including the stragglers, all looking at me. I know they just want to be milked, but I like to think there's more to it than that, that they're happy to see me, because I'm almost always happy to see them. My mother claimed cows were more intelligent than most people think, smarter than they themselves were willing to let on. It was all a plan, she told me when I was a little boy; someday, when no one was paying attention, all the cows from all over would get together and take over the world. So we'd better be nice to them, treat them like we'd like to be treated, because otherwise there'd be no more milk, cheese, ice cream. At the time I was most worried about the ice cream, but even after I was old enough to realize she was telling me a story, the idea stuck with me.

They were family, even if they did make me smell.

After my mother died, I wondered if they missed her, wondered why I was the one ringing the bell all the time now, why she no longer walked down the row and patted each of them on the head as the milking machines chugged away. I did the same things now, but sometimes it seemed like they looked at me like, *Yes, we know you, but where is she?* They were waiting, just as I was, for things to go back to normal, even though they never would.

Everything I know about milking cows I've learned from my mother: "stripping" a cow's teat to clean them out before milking, then cleaning the teat with iodine which used to sting my hands until I got used to it, wiping the teats clean, hooking everything up, the soothing sound of the milk going into the big tank, a sound that meant I'd done it right, a sound that would put Anna to sleep when she was fussy, because somehow my mother could hold Anna in one arm and do the milking with the other.

She used do the same thing with me, but of course I can't remember.

Letting the cows go would be like letting her go all over again. How could my father not see that? How could we not keep them?

My favorite time with milking is right now, when everything is running, the only sound the chuff chuff of the milking machines doing their work, and there's nothing to do but wait. Some of the cows will finish up sooner, some later...each one has their own rhythm, their own timing. Something else I learned from my mother.

I sit on an old wooden kitchen chair that belonged to my grandparents and that's been in the barn for as long as I can remember. When my father and I are both out here, we take turns, though why we don't just haul another chair out here so we can both sit, I don't know. The up and down, the sharing, that's part of the routine too. I put my hands behind my head and lean back, trying to look cool, like Andy did in class, invincible. But I lean too far back and almost go crashing to the hard cement floor before I catch myself. So much for invincible and cool. Andy's territory, not mine. Another fail, just like the picture I'd tried to draw, at trying to capture Andy.

Capture. What I was trying to do with Andy. Find a way to keep him, too, just like the cows. For what exactly, I wasn't sure. But I had to find a way.

5

Vicks VapoRub

"I don't know what you boys could possibly have to say to each other after spending the whole day in school together," my father says almost every night, after I ask if I can be excused from the table to use the telephone. "I'd think you'd be completely and totally talked out."

"We're in class all day," I say. "And there's just a few minutes in between." What I really mean is that we finally have time to talk, just him and me, with none of the other boys at the table going on and on about sports or seeing who can fart or belch the loudest while you're trying to eat your lunch.

It's the only time that I have Andy Olnan all to myself.

And we did always have things to talk about, still, a month after we met. Though it was Andy who did most of the talking, like he always did, and I listened, which is what I always did.

The first time Andy called me was the same day as the Kent Neustad rescue, after supper, just as we were finishing up.

"Hello?"

"Hi. Um, is Carl there?"

"This is him."

"It's Andy. Andy Olnan. From gym? I…helped you with your locker. I'm new?"

"Oh, hi." Did I sound casual enough?

"What are you doing?"

"Um, not much. Just getting to do some homework. You?" We were having a conversation. Outside of school. *He* called *me*. I was entering a new world, even if it was just for a few minutes.

"Not much. Watching some TV. Except my mom keeps yapping at me to do my math."

"Hm." Then I was stuck. *Come on! You're blowing it!*

"Um, do you know what we're supposed to do for geometry tomorrow? I forgot to write it down."

"The first five problems on page fourteen." At least I could be useful.

"Thanks. I'll be off in a minute! Knock it the hell off!" After that there were sounds of a scuffle, followed by a girl's voice making threats that I couldn't quite make out, then it was quiet. "Sorry about that. My sister. *Now* she wants to use the phone. Good thing I'm stronger than her." Andy laughed.

"Oh." I tried to picture Andy calling from his kitchen, or maybe the living room, a pesky sister, it seemed, trying to pull the phone away and him not giving up, hanging on tight, all so he could keep talking to me. "I sort of thought you'd have your own cell phone."

"I used to, in Minneapolis, but when we moved here my dad said I couldn't have one anymore. Part of the deal."

"What deal?"

"What?"

"You said it was part of a deal."

"Oh. Well, it's a long story. I'll tell you about it sometime."

"I don't have one either," I said.

"Why not?"

"That's a long story too." Something else we had in common, though I had a feeling his father's reasons didn't have anything to do with mine.

Then there was more commotion on the other end. "I said I'd give it to you as soon as I'm done. Now fuck off!" Then there was another female voice, this one sounding older, the three of them now arguing. "Sorry about that. My mom says I have to get off pretty soon. You got any sisters?"

"Just one. But she's only three."

"Lucky you. I'll bet she doesn't bug you when you're trying to talk on the phone."

"Not usually."

"Hm."

Then it was both of us just breathing. What now?

"Kent Neustad," Andy finally said. "What a complete and total asshole."

"I know. What an…asshole." For Andy the word came easily, just as it did for most of the other boys at school, but not for me. I wondered if my father heard me over the clatter of he and Ellen clearing the table and starting the dishes.

"A complete and total dickhead," Andy said, upping the ante. Was he testing me?

"Yup, definitely a dickhead." This time it rolled out smoothly and evenly, like I used it everyday. Maybe I just needed more practice.

"We need to think of some way to get back at him. Like… put Vicks VapoRub in his jockstrap or something."

Vicks VapoRub? But then it hit me, what it would feel like, that burning that I felt when I'd put some on my chest when I had a bad cold and couldn't breathe, except down there, Kent Neustad hopping around, mad as a hornet. We'd probably never get away with it, but even just the thought of revenge after all these years…too sweet to be true.

"I better go," Andy said. "Before my sister has a conniption. See you tomorrow." *Conniption.* Now that was a new one. I wanted to remember it to try out on my father, see how he'd react. *Sorry, Dad, I don't feel like doing the milking today, I'm in the middle of a conniption.* Certainly a lot safer than "dickhead."

"Sounds good." And then he was gone, before I had a chance to say goodbye, to say thanks for calling me. Could a boy thank another boy for calling and not have it be, well, too gay?

And so what if it was?

And our nightly conversations continue pretty much just like that: what happened at school, homework (Andy never wrote assignments down, but that didn't bother me; it was a reason for him to call), our awful sisters and how much they bugged us (that wasn't really true with Anna, since at three years old there isn't much that she does to annoy me, so I sometimes make up things to keep the conversation going). We never do get around to doing anything to Kent Neustad's jockstrap, but it's fun to talk about.

But keeping Andy all to myself couldn't last. By the end of September, Andy's become famous, like a prince with his own court. It started with his Mr. Osterman imitation and everyone asking him to do it just one more time, please stick your fingers up your nose again, it was too hilarious. And then he starts doing imitations of other teachers too, and before long he has a whole act put together.

Do Ms. Willman (the school nurse)! Andy has her pinched face and turned-up nose, when you tell her you want to get a pass to skip gym or go home, down pat.

Do Mr. Lindstrom (one of the custodians)! Andy saunters down the hall, waving people out of the way as he pretends to push a mop, yelling, "Coming through!" in Mr. Lindstrom's irritatingly nasal voice.

If Andy's a prince, I'm not sure what that makes me. A man in waiting? Whoever I am, I'm more than just an audience member. A manager, maybe? But whenever Andy does one of his imitations, he looks at me right afterward, with a "how did I do?" look, to see if it worked. I nod and smile, or I might even chime in with a "good job." And then he nods and smiles back at me, and everything feels perfect for that moment.

The problem is, it's just a moment. There's the rest of the day, including lunch, and there are fewer and fewer days when we sneak out, just him and me. Yes, it's too cold and rainy some of the time, but even on nice days Andy wants to stay in, and of course I agree. So we're back at the big table again, with the usuals, along with some hangers-on who get there too late and have to settle for the next table over, leaning over while they eat their soggy tacos and hoping to hear the conversation, which no matter what always seems to circle back to girls.

It isn't enough to just have a spontaneous conversation about them. It becomes, as Mr. Osterman might describe it if he was participating, a scientific inquiry. It always goes like this:

"Okay," Frank Willmert says. He always goes first. "Debbie Andersen."

"Debbie Andersen," Steve Thomsen says. It's his job to repeat the name.

"She's okay," Craig Franklin says. He's the "okay" guy. Every girl in the class is okay by him.

"Yeah, she's smart too," Ted Landsman says. He's the "brain" guy.

Brandon Williams, the "body" expert, frowns. "But they're not very big."

Ted concurs with his findings. "Nope, they're not. Not much there to do anything with."

"But would you do it with her?" Steve asks. He always gets the ultimate question.

"Maybe," Ted says.

"Probably," Frank says.

"Why not?" Brandon says.

Craig looks at Andy. "What do you think, Olnan?"

Andy pauses for a minute and looks at the ceiling, stroking an imaginary beard. Channeling Mr. Osterman? "I suppose if she was all that there was to pick from, maybe. Like if we were stranded on a desert island and we had to create a new civilization."

The other boys laugh and laugh, as if it's the funniest thing they'd ever heard, even though Andy's used it more than once, with some variations: If someone put a gun to my head, if I got paid lots of money, and so on. Whatever his take, he usually gets the last word.

A few days later, because we're apparently going through the list of girls in the class in alphabetical order, we're into the Ms.

"Cathy Martin."

And it's the same routine, everyone plays their part, Andy says something funny to sum it all up, I smile and eat and nod, relieved that I've slid by again.

"What about you, Paulsen?" Brandon asks. "You never say anything. You always just sit there."

"Yeah," Ted says. "She's your science partner. You must think something."

Frank's next. "Have you ever copped a feel? I know I would. They're huge."

Andy and I exchange a look. He nods a little, like he's encouraging me, but to do or say what I don't know.

"She's...nice," I say. "And smart. She does all the work. I'm getting an A in there."

There's silence, and then Ted shakes head and laughs. "Faggot," he says, under his breath, barely audible.

Andy sits up and leans over to him, his face just a few inches from Ted's. "*What* did you just say?"

"You heard me. Everybody knows it."

Everybody. My face is burning and I concentrate on taking the pickles off my tuna sandwich, even though I love pickles.

"Knows what?" Andy leans even closer.

"Nothing."

"You know what? You guys think you're such big Casanovas when you wouldn't know what to do with a girl if she came up right now and sat on your lap." Andy's winding up. "You couldn't find your... Oh, skip it."

Brandon puts up his hands. "Jeez. Calm down, Olnan. He didn't mean anything. If Paulsen just wants to sit there like...a lump, it's no skin off my butt." The other boys nod.

There are still a few *M*s to go, but no one picks it up after Cathy. "I gotta get to class," Andy says, getting up from the table. He pushes his chair in, hard, so that it bangs against the edge of the metal table, and walks away, fast, me trailing after him.

As we make the turn out of the cafeteria into the hallway I catch up to Andy and try to think of something to say. *What a bunch of dickheads?* Andy looks straight ahead, not at me.

"You can't just sit there," he says. "Otherwise, everyone's going to think— "

"Think what?" Even though I know exactly what he means.

"Never mind. Let's just get to class, okay?"

"Thanks for...you know." I can't seem to say *thanks for saving me again* even though that's what just happened. I don't want to feel like that's all we have in common.

He doesn't say *you're welcome*. He doesn't say anything at all.

"Who was Casanova?" I ask my father, who's sitting at the kitchen table, reading a *Modern Farmer* magazine with a jelly sandwich on white bread and a glass of milk in front of him. It's almost bedtime, and I'm having the same thing, making up for the dinner I couldn't eat much of earlier, the whole lunch-time incident sitting in my stomach like a stone.

He's already asked me, as he usually does, how my day went, and I said it was fine, nothing special, because of course there was no way I was going to go into it. So now I'm trying to make conversation, even though I have a pretty good idea about Casanova, because we're both just sitting there and the silence feels uncomfortable. And if my mind is on something else, then I don't have to think about what happened, what Ted Landsman said, what Andy said to me afterward.

My father looks up from the magazine and takes a bite of his sandwich. "Well, Casanova was supposedly the world's greatest lover. He had thousands of girlfriends during his lifetime."

"Really?"

"Well, I don't know if it was that many. But a lot. He hung around with royalty and other famous people so he was able to meet a lot of women."

"How do you know that?"

"Oh, some worthless information I must have picked up somewhere along the line. You know me. So why the interest in Casanova?"

I shrug my shoulders. "No reason. He...just came up in school today. Andy brought him up at lunch. We and some of the other guys were just talking about...girls and stuff, and... that was pretty much it."

My father smiles. "Ah, youth. Before long you guys will be driving up and down Main Street, looking for girls, and the girls will be looking for you. Except now I wonder if anyone even does that anymore. In person, I mean." He finishes his milk and sets the glass in the sink.

"It was just talk," I say. "It didn't really mean anything."

"You don't owe me any explanations. But someday soon,

before you know it, it'll be more than just talk. You have a lot
to look forward to. " He pats me on the shoulder. "Sleep well."

As I brush my teeth, wash my face, and get undressed for bed,
I wonder what's going to happen the next time we play the girl
game, and what I'm going to do.

Or if I even have to play at all.

I can't pretend.

But what if Andy can pretend and he's just better at it than
I am?

Where does that leave me?

Us?

6

SWEET SIXTEEN

It's late October, and I'm about to turn sixteen years old. "Sweet Sixteen," except that when you talk about a boy's sixteenth birthday you wouldn't include the "sweet" part, and there'd be no such thing as a "Sweet Sixteen" party like you might have if you were a girl, and who knows if that even happens now. I don't remember my mother ever talking about having a party when she turned sixteen; she was probably too busy doing farm work or homework to give it much thought.

The most important thing for me about being sixteen is finally getting my driver's license, which will be easy given that I've been driving since I was twelve, when my father started letting me drive the pickup on the gravel roads around the farm and eventually into town, though we'd pull over and switch before the city limits so he wouldn't get into trouble. The test: a no brainer. And then, I could borrow the pickup and escape Fullerton, even just for a few hours, with Andy Olnan.

Where would we go? Minneapolis? Maybe. But somewhere. Just him and me, and maybe once we're away we could finally talk about things, for real, without parents and chores and loud-mouthed boys talking about girls and what they'd do to them. We'd talk about what I feel about him, and I could ask him what he feels about me. Maybe I wouldn't like the answer, but at least I'd know.

For now we're in our routine, with school and talking on the phone. We still sit with the other boys at lunch and the girl game continues, but I've been let off the hook, at least for now, and it's like nothing ever happened. Andy chimes in just enough to show that he's one of them but not enough that he's committed to doing something and then reporting back, like some of the others have done, or claimed to have done. In other words, I'm not buying it when Brandon Williams says he was able to get his hands down someone's pants but then won't reveal any details about who, when, or where. I can tell by the way Andy rolls his eyes that he's thinking the same thing. Still, we sit with them anyway, as much as I wish we wouldn't. It's still a way to be with him.

Had I mentioned my birthday to him? If I did, it was lost in everything else during our nightly sessions: working out geometry problems together or trying to figure out what was going to be on a quiz in English, my father telling me for the fourth time to wrap it up, Andy's sister Joni in the background once again yelling that it was her turn for the phone, adding, *What is it with you? Are you a fag?* Then her laughing and then the silence between Andy and me, and then Joni gets off one final, parting shot: *You're supposed to like girls now.*

Who was she talking to? Andy, me, or both of us?

"Why don't we do something special for your birthday?" Ellen says at breakfast, a few days before the big event.

Though Ellen runs the house like it's a factory, she does do a great job with birthdays, compared to what it was like after my mother died and before Ellen moved in. Anna's was the first, and on her day, we had a store-bought cake that my father bought that was two days past its expiration date, and my father announced that just to make the occasion more special, we'd make it into a celebration of all three of our birthdays. He didn't say why, and I didn't ask, but I wondered if it was because, that way, we'd only have to think about birthdays once a year. But instead it just made my mother's absence even stronger, and even though that wasn't something my father and I seemed able to talk about, we both felt it. I could tell by the tentative way he cut into the cake, making Anna's slice way too big and mine just a sliver, and how he forgot to take the vanilla ice cream out of the freezer and we had to sit and wait for it soften enough to scoop onto the cake. Things my mother knew to do.

But now, with Ellen with us, birthdays come off like clockwork: I get chocolate with chocolate frosting (Ellen's favorite too), my father chocolate with white frosting (don't ask), and Anna, not being much of a cake fan, strawberry ice cream only. There are candles, wishes, we mumble through "Happy birthday," and we're done, an item checked off the list for another year. And then an hour or day or a week later, it always hits me what a birthday is, that you naturally have to think about who it is that made it possible for you to have one in the first place. Sometimes it seems like it's getting easier, which scares me because it's wrong to forget, and at other times it's harder, which scares me in a different way, because you know things will never be the same. "What did you have in mind?" I ask.

"Tell you what," my father says. "Why don't you invite your friend over? Spud's boy."

"Andy," I say, as if I need to make sure they know he's a real person, separate, not just the son of some guy with a weird nickname.

"Great idea," Ellen says. "What do you think?" All eyes are on me, even Anna's.

"I could ask him, I guess." Even though we've known each other for almost two months, neither of us has been to the other's house. We have our phone time and our school time, and while I wondered sometimes why he didn't invite me over, to be fair I hadn't done the same either. Would we just sit there in my room or his and talk about homework and Kent Neustad and the daily drudgery of everything just as we usually did?

Or could something actually *happen?*

Maybe a birthday party—would me, Andy, my father, Ellen, and Anna eating Ellen's hot dish and then cake constitute a party?—would be a good first step, never mind that someone else's idea of a great sixteenth birthday party would be a dozen other kids or more at the lake or in a basement, drinking beer or smoking a joint supplied by an older brother or sister or even a parent. I've never been invited to those types of parties, and as far as I know Andy hasn't been either. But would he think my party was pathetic, hokey, something only a friendless loser would do?

But I'm not friendless.

I have Andy, whether anything ever happens or not.

At least it's something.

Isn't it?

The next day, I wait for the right moment. But every time I get ready to ask, there's some interruption: some of the other boys hanging around Andy (but ignoring me as usual), time for our next class to start and me helping Andy finish the homework he should have gotten done the night before (also as usual). Finally, it's the end of the day, and the two of us are on the school bus. At his stop, Andy's almost to the door.

"Do you want to come over for supper on Wednesday for my birthday?"

"Sure," he calls back, the door closing on him, the bus starting to move.

Nothing to it.

For my birthday dinner, Ellen fixes my favorite hot dish of egg noodles, cream of mushroom soup, hamburger, and cheddar cheese, tossed salad with Thousand Island dressing, and chocolate cake with chocolate frosting. All things that my mother used to make, the recipes in a green metal box that I showed to Ellen not long after she moved in. She and I sat at the kitchen table and went through it, the ingredients in my mother's loopy and slanted handwriting, the cards sticky and stained with sauces, eggs, shortening. In the upper right-hand corner, my mother noted whether it was for a special occasion, and when we got to "egg noodle hot dish," there I was: CARL'S BD. "I'll have to remember that one," Ellen said, smiling. And of course she did, because she remembers everything.

My father said I could have the day off from chores since it's my birthday, but since I'm not sure what to do with the extra time, I end up helping anyway. The cows are expecting me, birthday or not.

But that's not it, not really.

I'm nervous about Andy coming, and I need something to

do to take my mind off it. What if they don't like him? Or he doesn't like them?

But even if that happened, would it make any difference?

After chores I put on a clean shirt and pants, help Ellen set the table, and wait by the front door for Andy. At just after six his mother pulls into our driveway, and my father and I go out to the steps to meet them. I've rehearsed the introductions over and over in my head: *Nice to meet you, Mrs. Olnan. This is my dad. Dad, this is Andy and his mom.* It would all be very polite and cordial. Except that Andy's mother doesn't get out of the car, and neither does Andy. The two of them sit there for what seems like a long time, Andy's mother talking and shaking and pointing her finger at him, Andy listening but staring straight ahead. Finally she gives him a little nudge and he gets out of the car, Mrs. Olnan not even waving to us as she drives away.

Just as I'm about to finally do introductions my father steps in.

"You must be Andy. I'm Carl's dad. It's nice to meet you." My father puts out his hand and Andy takes it.

"Nice to meet you too. Thank you for inviting me." Then it's the smile, first for my father, then for me. My shoulders, which I must have been holding up against the bottom of my ears, can now come down. *This is going great!*

"Your dad and I go way back. We were friends at Fullerton High, same class. Looks like you boys are carrying on the tradition."

"I know. He told me that you guys knew each other."

"To tell you the truth, I was surprised to hear you were heading back down here to farm your grandma's place. Seems like your dad was doing something with computers up there. Is that right?"

"Uh-huh." Andy looks uncomfortable, anxious, not sure where to look, not sure what to do with his hands.

"Must be a bit of an adjustment to leave the big city, then settle here. Lots going on up there, right?"

"Yup."

"Kind of a tough time to start farming. But I'm sure he

must know what he's getting into. Your friend here can give you lots of tips about doing chores." My father tilts his head at me and winks. That surprises me since he's never been much of a winker.

"He…just wanted to do something different." Finally, a complete sentence. "That's all. My mom too."

"Well, hope it all works out for you folks, and we're glad you're back home. I know Carl is. Aren't you, Carl?"

"Yup." Now I'm the one who can't think of more to say.

After some more awkward silences we finally sit down to supper. I'm still waiting for the Andy from school, the king of tenth grade, to appear. *This isn't him,* I want to say. *This is an imposter.* I'm sorry for him and embarrassed by him at the same time.

My father tries again with more questions about Minneapolis. "What kinds of things did you like to do up there?"

"Um, I don't know. Stuff, I guess."

Stuff?

But then it occurs to me that, despite all the time we've spent together, Andy hasn't said a whole lot about *what* he did when he lived there. I hadn't really thought about him…doing things. Having friends, hanging out. I just assumed that he did. Unlike me, he seemed good at that sort of thing. Maybe I was just glad he'd picked me and I didn't care about anything else.

"Sports?"

"Nope, not really."

"Music?"

He shakes his head.

"What about your folks?"

Andy frowns, like he hasn't quite heard.

"What kinds of things did they do in the Cities?"

Either my father is really nosy, or just desperately trying to get Andy to talk about something, anything. At this point it doesn't matter to me, just so long as it works.

"A lot of church stuff. That's about it."

"Well, you all are going to be plenty busy soon," my father

says, passing Andy the salad. "Believe me, we know." Another wink. *But Andy doesn't plan to do chores,* I'm thinking. *Andy, remember what you said about slavery and all that?* I can only imagine what my father would do with that, and Andy's flaming out as it is. Best to let it go, and hope someone changes the subject. But instead there's more quiet, the only sound our utensils scraping against plates. Finally, Ellen comes to the rescue.

"Do you have any little sisters at home, Andy?"

Andy looks up from his plate. "No, just an older one."

"Do you hate earth science as much as Carl does?"

"It's okay."

"Just okay? Aw, come on. You seem like a pretty smart guy. I bet it's a breeze for you."

Andy shrugs his shoulders and says nothing, but for the first time since we sat down, there's a little bit of smile, the same smile he's used on me.

"Mr. Osterman is a strange guy sometimes."

Ellen laughs. "Tell me about it. He was that way when I had him too."

"Wow. He's been around a long time," Andy says. "I mean, it's not like you're *that* old, it's just that…" He blushes.

Ellen reaches over, touches his hand, and smiles. "No worries. I'm just a bit older than you two, but not by much."

Ellen laughs, then Andy laughs, my father laughs, and with that the ice is broken. I laugh too, just so I'm not left out. Andy even starts asking my father questions. *Is it hard to milk a cow? What was it like being a teacher?* But before long his attention shifts completely to Ellen: *What did you like in school? Have you always lived in Fullerton? What's your favorite TV show? This tastes really good, what did you put in it? I wish my mom would make stuff like this.*

And on and on it goes. My father and I sit and watch, total bystanders. He winks at me, again, though I don't really understand why. Maybe he thinks it's funny the way Andy is talking to Ellen, like one grown-up to another. I'm trying hard to see the good side of it: at least Andy came, and he finally seems happy about it. But it's not because of me.

After the cake and the ice cream I open my presents: from Ellen there's a new shirt and sweater—from the young men's section of Penney's in Mankato, not the boy's, she points out—and from my father and Anna twenty dollars for me to spend on whatever I want. Andy apologizes for not bringing anything. "My mom was supposed to take me to town to get something, but she had to do a thing at the church," he says.

"That's okay," I say. "You came over." *That was enough of a present*, I want to add, but I know I don't dare say it. Not out loud. Too gay.

"That Andy sure is a talker," my father says. We're on our way home in the pickup after dropping him off. "Once you get him started."

"I know," I say, even though I'm not really listening. I'm thinking about how tomorrow would just be another day, no presents, no favorite hot dish, nothing really special at all. There'd be no Andy at the dinner table, even if he didn't pay all that much attention to me. At least he was there.

"Guess Ellen must just bring out the best in him." My father laughs. "I'd say he's a little smitten with her, if you ask me."

"Smitten?"

"I think he might have a little crush on her. Kinda cute, don't you think?"

Wait a minute.

Andy is supposed to be having the crush on me. That's the plan. "He was just trying to be nice."

"Maybe. But boy, did his eyes light up when she started paying some attention to him. Didn't you notice?"

"Not really." But of course I'm lying, and I realize I might have made a huge mistake.

The next day, Andy's waiting for me, pacing back and forth in front of my locker.

"So what did she say about me?"

Nothing about thanks for having me over, it was fun, sorry again that I didn't bring a present.

"Who?"

"You know. That girl that lives with you."

"Ellen?" I have to think. What *had* she said?

"You mean she didn't say anything about me? Not anything?" He looks at me, his face scrunched up, like something hurts. This must be what *smitten* looks like.

"She's a lot older than you, you know. *A lot.*"

"Not that much older. A couple years. Maybe three or four at the most. But I think she sorta liked me back. Didn't you think that?"

"Well, she said you had a good appetite. She liked it that you ate a lot." That was true. While Ellen and I were doing the dishes and my dad took Andy out to see the cows, she'd commented on what a "good eater" he was. "I thought he might ask for thirds," she'd said, laughing.

"That was it?" Andy looks down at his shoes and sighs. "That I ate a lot?"

"Well, there was one other thing," I say, even though there really *is* nothing else. But that doesn't mean I can't make something up.

"What?" His eyes grow wide.

"Well, she thought you were nice." It isn't a lie, not really, even though she never said that about Andy, not exactly. But I was sure she would have, if I'd asked.

"Nice?" Andy looks at the floor again. Nice wasn't going to cut it, either.

"And that you were cute."

"Really?" For the first time this morning, Andy smiles. "That I was cute?"

I nod. I hope that by just merely agreeing and not saying it out loud again, I can make the lie not quite as bad, even though I know that it doesn't work that way.

"Cute *and* nice," Andy says. "Not bad."

I nod again. I've taken this too far, I know. But I know what I'm doing.

I've got a plan.

Because all of this stuff about Ellen is just him trying to be like everybody else, to fit in at the lunch table.

If it takes a little bit of lying (well, maybe more than a little bit) to keep him until he's ready, then I'm willing to do it.

Keep him. Like he's a piece of clothing, or a pet? But it's more than that. I want him to keep me, too.

And ready for what?

Ready to see that he and I should be one another's another.

7

MACARONI AND CHEESE

"There's nothing to DO out here," Andy sighs. "Except for these stupid chores."

It's one of the last nice days of autumn, still warm enough to lie on the grass, so Andy and I stretch out on our backs in the narrow yard alongside his house, our hands tucked behind our heads.

Even though we're supposed to be doing Andy's "chores" and we haven't even started them yet, Andy says we deserve a break. Never mind that he said he wasn't going to do any chores to begin with. His father apparently had something else to say about that. I'd never say it to Andy, and I'm sorry, but the things he has to do aren't real chores. Those won't happen until they actually plant something next spring, and since they haven't decided if they're going to have any stock, no cows to milk or hogs to feed either yet. Having to rake a few leaves or take out the recycling just isn't in the same league as farm chores, and I'm pretty sure that other farm kids would agree with me. What makes chores "chores" is that they are things you can only do on a farm and that take a little bit of skill and strength, like milking, growing crops, taking care of animals. And, I suppose, that they can make you smell. Part of the deal. Everything else is, well, upkeep. No different than what any town kid might have to do on a fall Saturday afternoon.

For once I don't have to worry about *my* chores, since Andy's invited me for supper and Ellen says not to worry, she and my father are on it. It was really Andy's mother who'd done the inviting: *My mom says you should come and eat with us since you had me over for your birthday. So she said to come over on Tuesday. Okay?* But it didn't matter that the invitation had come secondhand, and that Andy, unlike me and my birthday dinner, probably hadn't spent much time trying to figure out the best way to do it. I get out of chores for a day and I get to be with Andy. Everything is perfect.

"Why do they call them chores?" Andy asks me.

"I don't know. They just do."

"What a stupid word. Makes me feel like I'm an ox or something. You know?"

"Yeah, I know," I say again, even though I'd never thought about it like that. Chores were what you did, what your job was. I'd never known anything different. But agreeing with whatever Andy says has become a habit.

"I hate it here," Andy says. "Goddamn my grandma for leaving us this crappy place and goddamn my stupid-ass father for bringing us to it. Everything was perfect up there. But of course no one gives a flying fuck what I think." Among the many things that I like about Andy is the way he swears, the way the words come out of Andy's mouth, the hardness of the Ds and the Fs and the Gs, even though I'd been brought up to believe that any type of swearing that used God's name was, while not necessarily resulting in eternal damnation, certainly frowned upon in the Lutheran way of thinking.

"So why did he? Make you move down here, I mean. If everything was okay."

"He had his reasons. I mean they. My mom was in on it too, right from the beginning." He shakes his head and looks away. "And they got my sister to go along with it. So it was three against one."

"So why does he want to farm, if he already had a job and everything?" I sound like my father, not that I really care why they came. Andy is here. That is the main thing. I'm thinking of my father and how he'd probably pump me as soon as I got home for some dirt on what was going on at the Olnan place, what was Spud thinking, blah, blah, blah. I figure it couldn't hurt to be prepared.

"They had their reasons. It was like…" Then he's off in the distance, somewhere else.

"Like what?"

"Like they really didn't give a shit what I wanted. But since when do parents ever do that? And just because…"

As much as I like Andy, I get a little bit impatient with these incomplete sentences, like we're in the middle of a psychological exam or something. "Because what?"

Andy shakes his head. "Skip it."

"Okay." A dead end. So I try relating, even though I hate that word. It's so…what? New agey, I guess. "I know what you mean, though. My dad keeps talking about getting rid of the farm, even though we've had it forever. He doesn't really care what I think. He just wants to do what he wants. But what are you going to do? Parents are, well, parents." That was profound. But at least I'm trying. "Know what I mean? In the end, they don't really care." But is that really true of my father, or am I just saying that for Andy's benefit? I'm not sure how I feel about making my father look bad, even though we might disagree, just to look good to Andy.

But whatever my intentions are, Andy doesn't pick up on my attempt to empathize, to try to relate, or to see what my story is. That's Andy, and I'm willing to overlook it because, well, it's Andy. "If we had to move, why couldn't we move to someplace halfway interesting? If Minneapolis is so evil, why not Duluth? Then we could live on that big lake. What's it called?"

"Lake Superior."

"You ever been there?"

"Nope. What's so evil about Minneapolis?"

Andy ignores my question. "I looked it up on a map. It's like an ocean. If we'd moved there, then my dad could have been a fisherman. Or a sailor on a ship. Then he'd be gone a lot. That would be sweet. Anything but some dumb-assed farmer." Andy sits up and leans back on his elbows. "We should go see it. That'd be cool, don't you think?"

"How would we get there?" I can't help being practical, Andy or no. It's the way I am.

"I don't know. Hitchhike, maybe, or take a train. We'd find a way." Andy lies back down, sighs, and closes his eyes.

We are a *we*. The two of us. A couple. Of course friends can go places together, and maybe that is all he really means. But then I picture us on a train, at nighttime, our reflections together in the window, holding hands under a blanket, two boys on an adventure, running away from chores, both real and not real, our inconsiderate fathers, and the Kent Neustads of the world.

I turn on my side so I can look at him. I study his Adam's apple and the short, pale blond hairs that sprout up from it in a perfect line. Then suddenly Andy turns too, so that we're facing each other. "What?"

"Nothing." I lie back down. "We really should finish up your chores." I stand and brush off the back of my jeans.

Andy holds out his hand. "Help me up, man."

I take Andy's hand and pull him to his feet, but I don't let go right away. Andy holds on too, and even though it's just for a couple of extra seconds, his hand feels warm in mine, just like it would on the train to Duluth.

Andy's mother fixes macaroni and cheese out of a box for supper, something I've never had before, and peanut butter sandwiches. She's about a head and a half shorter than Andy, with short blond hair like his except it's starting to go gray at the roots. She seems a little frazzled, talking a mile a minute and apologizing as she dumps the noodles into the boiling water. It's all she can manage, she says, after a full day of volunteer cleaning at Redeemer Baptist Church, which they've recently joined since moving to town, leaving no time for shopping and making a proper home-cooked meal.

"Such nice people there," she says to me. "Everyone's been so nice since we've come back to town. Such a blessing to be making new friends, along with seeing some old ones. Makes it easier to start over fresh. Wouldn't you say so, Andy?"

"Hm," he says. He looks at me and rolls his eyes.

"And I'm so glad Andy has made a friend." She smiles at me and stirs the macaroni, her face shiny from the steam. "Andy needs that so much. Good, solid friends."

"I'm glad too," I say. "It must be hard to be new. I mean, even when you've lived here before. It's like being new all over again, I suppose."

"What a smart thing to say." She pats my arm. "Why, yes, it is. Tell me, Carl, where do you folks go to church?"

"Calvary," I say. "Just outside of town." I leave out the part about how we only go during major holidays now, since my mom died.

"Oh," she says, disappointed. "There's a very nice youth group at Redeemer that I would love for Andy to join, and if you went there too, then the both of you could go and—"

"I wouldn't drag my worst enemy to that loser group."

"That's enough, Andrew. You've made your feelings on that subject very clear. But I don't think it would hurt you to at least try it."

"I'm not going!"

"We're not going to argue about it now, not in front of company. Let's all sit down."

Joni, Andy's sister and our telephone tormentor, is working on a school project with a friend so won't be eating with us, his mother explains. "Big loss," Andy says, rolling his eyes and flipping his hair. I just smile, but secretly I'm glad she won't be here to do more of her name calling, which would probably be a lot more embarrassing in person than over the telephone. And Andy's father is back in Minneapolis, Andy's mother explains, still wrapping things up from the business, and won't be back until later the next day. "Lucky bastard," Andy mutters, which is quickly followed by an "Andrew!" from his mother.

After we sit down, the three of us join hands to say the grace. I'm hoping it will be a long prayer, so I can hang on to Andy, and it is. After thanking and blessing everything under the sun, each time it seems like Andy's mother is about to wrap it up, she takes off again. Finally, she gets to what sounds like the end: "And finally, in addition to blessing this food, oh Lord, please bless our guest at this table, Carl, for his friendship and for joining us at our table in worship and in fellowship and

continue to guide us on our journey towards purity and obedi-
ence and give us the strength to resist temptation and evil. In
the name of Jesus Christ, Amen."

"If that had gone on any longer, it'd be time to eat breakfast
tomorrow," Andy says. He looks at me and rolls his eyes again.

At first, just like when Andy was at our house, no one says
anything as the three of us eat. Andy's mother hovers and fuss-
es, refilling our glasses with more milk, adding more macaroni
and cheese to our plates without us asking, putting more white
bread out for our sandwiches. Then, as Andy and I are finishing
up our third helpings, his mother turns to me with a pained
look on her face. "So how are you all doing, Carl?"

"I'm fine. Getting kind of full, though. Everything tastes
really good."

"I mean at your place. With your family and such. I know
that you all have been through a lot the last few years. Even
though we were up in Minneapolis I still kept up on all the
Fullerton goings on, you know."

"We're fine," I say. "We're good." Even though of course
that isn't really true, with my father and his talk about getting rid
of the farm because we're going broke. I figure that he wouldn't
take it too well if I spilled the beans about that, especially when
his archrival Spud Olnan would be sure to hear about it from
Mrs. Olnan. Best to be noncommittal.

"Well, I sure do wish I'd gotten to know your mother better
when I lived here. Your dad too. Andy's dad always thought
highly of your dad, being a teacher and everything. I'm sure it
can't be easy for you all, especially with the little one. They've
sure done a nice job of raising a good boy like you." She reaches over and squeezes my wrist. "And God has a way of giving
us strength when we most need it to do the things that we need
to do. He has certainly done that for us, hasn't He, Andrew?"

"Thank you," I say. Or maybe I am supposed to say "amen."
My face feels hot, and I wish she'd change the subject.

"And good thing you have that Hansen girl to look after you
folks."

Andy kicks me under the table and giggles.

Andy's mother frowns at him. "What's so funny?"

"Nothing. Carl likes Ellen, that's all. I mean he *really* likes her." He kicks me again, this time harder. I give him a *knock it off* kick back, but he just smiles.

"Well, I'm sure he does. She's a nice young woman, from what I've heard."

"Oh, she is," Andy says. "Real nice." He makes his hands into fists, puts them under his sweatshirt and pushes them out. Then he looks at me and laughs. I try to laugh, too, but nothing comes out. All I can manage is a half smile. Mrs. Olnan reaches across the table and slaps him on his cheek with the back of her hand. It's hard enough to make a sound, but Andy doesn't let on. "That's rude, Andrew." He does it again, but this time his mother ignores him and starts clearing the table.

I stand up and push my chair in. "Can I help?"

"Aren't you a polite boy. See that, Andrew? Pay attention to your friend here and his manners. No thanks, honey, I can manage." She squirts dishwashing soap into the sink. "I think there's some vanilla ice cream in the freezer if you boys are interested."

"Maybe later," Andy says. "Let's go up to my room. I wanna show you something."

"You sure you don't want help?"

"You boys go on. But thanks anyway, honey. You're sweet."

At the bottom of the stairs, just as we're about to go up, Andy grabs my arm. "What's with all this polite crap?"

"What do you mean?"

"'Can I help? Shouldn't we help with the dishes?' Jeez." He says it in a high, girlish voice, and it's embarrassing to think I might sound that way to other people, even just a little bit.

"I just thought I'd ask. Don't you usually help your mom?"

"Not if I can help it. And you shouldn't either. It makes me look bad."

"Sorry. I was just trying to be nice."

"Next time, don't be so nice."

"Well, what else could I do? Especially after she put me in the prayer and everything."

Andy snorts. "Her and her hour-long prayers. Once you're in them, you're in for life. Believe me, I know. It's 'save Andy from this, save Andy from that' every damn night of the week."

"What exactly do you need saving from?"

"Everything, according to her. Come on."

When we get to his room Andy closes the door. "Wait till you see this," he whispers. He lifts up the bedspread and slides his arm between the mattress and the box spring, all the way up to his shoulder. "Talk about a pain in the butt. But my mom likes to snoop around too much." He pulls out a magazine without a cover and hands it to me.

"I found it when I was out burning the trash the other day. It has to be my dad's. You're not going to believe this." Andy takes the magazine, turns it over and shakes it until one of the pages falls into my lap. It's a picture of a woman sitting on a green velvet couch, with her index finger up to her lips, like she's telling someone to be quiet. She has long black hair, dark eyes, thick lips that are painted bright red. She's wearing a pair of shiny black heels, a string of white pearls, and nothing else. The picture is smudged and wrinkled, and the crease in the middle has been taped to hold everything together. "So what do you think?"

"She's...naked," I say.

"Duh." Andy points at her breasts. "Look how gigantic they are."

"You must look at her a lot."

"She's my best girl." The way Andy says it is soft, dreamy, like he's in love. "So who do you think she looks like?"

"I don't know. Some girl, I guess."

Andy frowns. "Don't you see it?"

I stare at the picture, trying to focus on her face, but my eyes keep moving to her breasts, her small waist, the small triangle of hair between her legs. I've never seen a naked woman's whole body before. It's not like I've ever wanted to, but there it is.

"Well?"

I shake my head. "It's just some girl."

"It's her," he says. "That must be what she looks like. It has to be."

"Who?"

"Your maid, you dipshit."

"Ellen?"

"You got another maid I don't know about?"

I don't like him calling Ellen our maid. A maid is a middle-aged woman who wears a black-and-white uniform and a funny-looking hat, like in the movies.

And now that I'm getting used to the woman in the picture, I can see that she doesn't look anything at all like Ellen: her hair is too long, and Ellen's lips are much thinner, and besides that I've never seen Ellen without any clothes, so how would I—or Andy—know whether the woman really looks like her or not?

"Doesn't she give you a boner?" Andy smiles and presses on his crotch. "Every time I look at her I get one. And not just your average hard on. A *major* one."

"Hm," I say, trying to be noncommittal, even though the truth is I don't feel anything anywhere when I look at her. Except maybe sadness. And mostly for Andy. It's all part of the act: the "crush" on Ellen (the real one), the stuff with the kicking and the boobs when we were having supper, and now this stupid picture. Andy's act. If he can convince me that he likes girls, maybe then he can convince himself.

But if Andy wants her to be Ellen, then she'll be Ellen. I just need to be a little patient, go along, until Andy realizes what's going on. Between him and me. All this guy stuff about naked girls and pictures and boobs won't mean anything in the end. I'm willing to wait for as long as it takes.

"I'll make a deal with you. Because you're my buddy, I'm gonna let you borrow her. Not for good, but for a little while."

"If you really want to keep her, that's okay." I'm trying to find a way out, a way not to have anything more to do with her than I already have. It's one thing to agree with him, but it's another to actually have to keep the picture, even if it's just a loan.

Andy frowns. "Don't you want her? I'm trying to be a pal here."

I feel trapped. "Well, it's just that you really like her, and I don't want to take her from you if—"

"But I'm willing to share. That's what guys do. You know?"

I don't say anything, because I know I'm stuck. Whenever I look at it, I'll think of Ellen, even though it isn't her, and I don't like the idea of her being stuck naked in a photograph that's been looked at so much that it's torn down the middle and has to be taped back up again. But I needed to look at the larger picture. It's a way to keep us together. "Well, if you're sure…"

"But you have to promise something first."

"What?"

"You have to *promise* to take really good care of her. Because she's my girl, you know." Andy folds the picture up again and puts it in my hand, gently, like it's a piece of glass, or an egg.

I take her because Andy wants me to, and this way I'll at least have something of his, even if it's only an old faded picture of a naked woman he's in love with because it reminds him of a real person.

"I promise," I say. "I'll guard her with my life."

8

HOG PENS

When I get home from Andy's, I put my bike in the shed next to the barn, reach into my back pocket, and feel around for Ellen, to make sure she's still there.

I sneak past the real Ellen, busy making supper in the kitchen, and head up to my room. I don't think I can talk to her right now, or really, even look at her. Not after what I've been up to at Andy's. I feel like she could see right through me, to my insides, and somehow know, and it makes me feel like I should stand under a hot shower for half an hour.

I sit down at my desk and unfold the picture, careful not to tear her. When I turn on the lamp I can see Andy's fingerprints smudged on her, on her breasts, between her legs. I wonder what he thinks about at those moments when he touches her, if he says things to her, what he imagines her saying to him in reply.

I can see stains on the paper too. From Andy. I picture him in bed, at night, his hand moving up and down, her next to him, in just the right place so he can see everything. He goes back and forth between the picture Ellen and the real Ellen, trying to bring them together into one person. He thinks about her just as I think about him, when the house is quiet, and I'm alone, my hands under the covers. I put my fingers there, where his have been, to see if it'll help me feel what Andy feels. But I don't feel anything, except the worn-out paper. And maybe Andy doesn't feel anything either. Maybe it's all part of him trying to change who he is, hoping that a worn-out picture from an old magazine will somehow change things.

I take out my catalog, stick the picture in the middle in the same page as the man, and put it back under the bed. Maybe they'll become friends. Andy and I each have our own pictures, it seems, though it doesn't seem like we like the same person. Probably not a good sign, but too soon to give up. My plan is to keep her long enough that Andy will start to miss her and want her back, but in the meantime I'd like nothing better than to forget about her, at least for a while. And if Andy asks how things went with her, I'll be enthusiastic but vague. "Great!" I'll say, and then put her back in his hands just as he'd put her in mine.

After she's tucked safely away, I go looking for my father, to help with the rest of chores. He's in the barn, looking at Rebecca, one of the cows.

"Where've you been? I was about ready to give up on you." He sounds a little owly.

"I ate at Andy's, remember?"

"So does Spud Olnan have any clue about what he's doing?" Nothing about how was supper, what did you have, how is Andy doing, does he still have a thing for Ellen.

"Well, they haven't done anything yet. They're just sort of… living there right now."

My father turns away from Rebecca and looks at me. "Well, that's real smart. Buy a farm and then not doing anything with it." His voice is sharp, with an edge that I'm not used to. I've touched a nerve, but I have no idea why.

"Well, I suppose they're going to wait until spring to plant." It looks like what it is, a farm: there's some buildings, room for animals, a yard, a house (a messy one, but his mom worked all day, and not everybody is lucky enough to have an Ellen). "Andy's dad—I mean Spud—is still working up in the Cities part of the time."

My father frowns and shakes his head. "Well, he probably realizes he's in way over his head. Farming isn't just something you get into overnight. Though I suppose it doesn't hurt if your mother leaves you a sweet deal like he has. He's never worked a day of his life on a farm, and now he's sitting on one of the best spreads in the county just because he has a relative in the business. And no clue what to do with it."

"Well, it seemed to me like..." I say it slowly, trying to buy time. "Well, it looks to me like the pen he's got is going to be way too small for the number of hogs he might want." It's a lie, because they aren't going to even have hogs, but I like how smoothly I can say it, how clear and logical it sounds. And most important, it gives my father a chance to be an expert on something other than dairy cows, and maybe that will help him get out of his funk. "They're pretty crowded in there, and if he ever gets more he's going to have a big problem."

"See?" my father says. "That's exactly what I mean." He takes off his work gloves and cracks his knuckles, something he always does when he feels satisfied that he's won an argument. "You don't just waltz in, start raising hogs, like you've been doing it your whole life when you haven't. That's what makes a good farmer. It's on-the-job training."

We don't even raise hogs, so who are you to tell Spud Olnan what to do? And besides that, who showed you everything there was to know about cows?

Mom.

But I let it go. Whether my father likes Andy's father doesn't matter, not really. What matters is what's between Andy and me.

"I'm not sure what's going on with this one," my father says, thankfully changing the subject. He pats Rebecca's head, looking worried. She's always been one of the sicklier ones in our herd, and because of that we have a soft spot for her. That happens when you're around cows all the time, and you realize that without them, you wouldn't eat, have clothes, have a home. And it sounds corny, I know, but they're like family, like extra children that you care for and worry about. They become everything. So if Rebecca takes a little longer to come in for milking, that is fine, and while I talk to all of the cows, I am always sure to take some extra time to tell her that she is a good girl. "She didn't give me hardly anything today. I'm wondering if maybe she's done."

"For good?"

My father shrugs his shoulders. "Hard to tell."

Every so often, a cow will dry up and no longer give milk, even though by all appearances she seems fine. There isn't much we can do but "send her away." Those were the words my mother would use. When I was five, Maggie, my favorite at the time, disappeared one day and according to mother would not be coming back. I convinced myself that she was simply going on a vacation, or perhaps to a zoo, where she would live out her days with lots of grass to eat, time to rest from years of milking, children petting the big brown spot between her eyes as I used to do.

As I've gotten older, it's become easier to see them go, because I understand that some things simply come down to money. We couldn't keep a cow that wasn't doing her job. Still, when the truck came to take her, I busied myself with something else, leaving the goodbyes to my mother, who sent them on their way and then got back to work. It wasn't that she didn't care; there just wasn't time to be sad because there was so much else to do. The cows that we had, the healthy ones, needed our attention.

But I don't really know if any of that—learning to say goodbye, I mean—helped me much with her own death. I found myself thinking as I did when I was six years old: like the cows, she was just going away, for a little vacation, but unlike the cows, she'd be coming back. That was what my father had told me. At first it didn't matter that the trips got longer and longer each time, and when she did finally come home, she seemed worse off than the time before. She might get a little worse before she got better, my father had said. But weren't hospitals supposed to make you better? Whatever they were doing, it didn't seem to be working. And then, finally, she too was gone.

I had known it was cancer, and because it had spread quickly there wasn't much they could do. But it wasn't until after she died that I learned exactly what had happened. *Women's cancer*, I had overhead some of the neighbor women talking about it in the church kitchen as they sliced brownies and put out the lunchmeat and scooped macaroni salad for the lunch after the funeral. I'd gone in for a glass of water for Anna and they hadn't seen me. *Once it's into your female parts, it's all over,* one whispered to another. And then they were talking about someone else whose cancer was similar to my mother's, comparing how long the other mother had lasted compared to mine. They just smiled at me when they finally noticed me standing there, as if I couldn't possibly know what they were talking about, even though I understood every word.

But it didn't really matter.

Animals and mothers get sick, animals and mothers die. Maybe it is wrong to tie the two things together, but it's what I go back to when I miss her and I'm trying to understand.

"Do we need to call Doc Winter?" Dr. Winter is our vet, and I make a point of calling him "Doc" because that's how my father refers to him, even though it's a bit hokey, like something out of an old movie, and I use "we" as well, because it makes me feel like it's my decision, too, about what to do.

"Let's keep an eye on her for a day or two, see if she snaps out of it on her own." My father throws his gloves on the ground. "Maybe we should just sell the goddamn things. Do something else that doesn't take so much work. A visit from the vet just to look at her, never mind anything else—hell, that's a hundred dollars right there. Just to drive all the way out here and tell us to keep an eye on her. Crops don't need doctors. You just plant them and watch them grow. Or let's just get out completely while the getting's good."

"There's hail," I try. "And what if it doesn't rain? Or it rains too much? There's weeds."

My father sighs and shakes his head. "We've been over this before."

He's right, of course. We have been. "You wouldn't really, would you?" *They're her cows,* I want to say. *Not yours.* But I don't. It's ammunition I think I should save for later.

My father doesn't answer.

Ellen's in the kitchen drying the dishes, with Anna on the floor with my old Tinkertoys, her new favorite thing to play with. No matter what, she always has to be in the kitchen when Ellen is working, even if it means everyone else has to step over her. In the time that Ellen's been with us, they've become inseparable, which is only natural, I suppose, though I sometimes wonder if Anna's memory of our mother will soon fade away to nothing and be replaced by Ellen. For a while I took it upon myself to try to ensure that wouldn't happen. I'd show Anna pictures of our mother, including pictures of Anna with her, in her arms. I'd point to our mother, and say, slowly, enunciating every syllable as if I were teaching her a foreign language, "This is our mother. *Moth-er.*" But Anna would look at me with a blank stare. I'd try again. "*Moth-er.*" "El," she would finally say, the letter easier than sounding out the whole name. That was who she wanted. When your mother leaves you at two, how could she be anything but a strange blond woman, smiling for the camera? It was then that I knew I'd have to be content with just my memories, and not try inventing them for Anna.

I pour myself a glass of milk and sit down at the table. Ellen puts down the dishrag and sits across from me. "Rebecca sick again?"

"It looks like it. We're going to see if she gets better before we call the vet. Dad…"

"Your dad what?"

"Nothing. He's just being…" I can't find the right word. "Stubborn?"

"Hm. He probably just wants to keep an eye on her for now. Expensive to get a vet out here if you don't have to."

"I know."

"How was supper with your friend? Was it fun?"

"It was okay. We had macaroni and cheese. The box kind." I'm not sure what else I can tell her. *And then we looked at a picture of a naked girl that looks just like you. Or at least Andy thinks she does. He gave her to me. To keep for a while so I can look at her some more. She's upstairs, hiding. But she doesn't look anything like you. She's just a picture, but you're real.*

"Did I spill something?" Ellen looks down, then at me. I

realize I'd been staring at her breasts, making comparisons, trying to see what Andy sees.

"Um, nope, I was just thinking again…"

"About your dad and the cows?"

"Yeah, I suppose." But not really. I'm thinking about Andy, and Andy thinking he wanted Ellen or just any girl in general, and me wanting Andy, but not being sure what to do about it. Knowing that sooner or later everything was going to collide, one way or another.

Ellen laughs. "You know, for a kid, you sure do think a lot. I'd ease up a little, try not to get too carried away worrying about the future." As I've said before, Ellen may be all business, but she also knows what's going on, at least with my father. She picks up Anna, gently pulls the Tinkertoy stick out of her mouth that she's been chewing on, and wipes her face. "It'll all work out."

It's the same thing my mother had said, when everything inside me started to change, a couples of months before died. She was home then, in bed pretty much all of the time, her face round and puffy and red from medications to help her keep food down, her head bald from the chemotherapy. Anna was spending nearly every day with neighbors and most nights, while my father and I took turns in between chores taking care of my mother. We were getting by on lunch meat sandwiches and the occasional hot dish dropped off by the women from church, my mother on canned chicken noodle soup and saltine crackers. One late afternoon, not long before she died, a Tupperware bowl on her lap for her nausea, the two of us sat with nothing except the sound of her breathing between us.

"What are you thinking?" That was something she often asked me whenever I was unusually quiet, when she knew I had something on my mind. I often replied with a shrug of my shoulders or a *nothing much*, but she rarely let that be the end of it. "Tell me."

"I'm scared." *There.* For once I was out with it. No cajoling necessary. If ever there was a time for honesty, and to be quick about it, it was then.

The doctors had said it could happen anytime.

My mother looked at me, straight on but with some softness in her eyes. "What about?"

"Everything."

She nodded. "What's everything?"

"You...leaving us," I said, as if she were going on a long vacation by herself and might not come back. "Leaving me." I couldn't say *dying*, not yet.

She nodded again. "Of course you'd feel that way. This is hard for all of us. Is there something else?"

"Isn't that enough?"

But somehow she knew there was more, just as she knew when I was small and I would lie about breaking something or taking the last piece of cake. *The cover up is almost always worse than the crime.*

"I think there might be something wrong with me." I wasn't sure how else to put it. "About how I feel."

My mother coughed and took a sip of water. "There's nothing wrong with how you feel."

"How do you know what I'm talking about?" But yet I knew that she knew. Dying could do that for a person: getting to the heart of it.

"I just know. Mothers know things." She smiled but started coughing again, this time a bone-rattling cough that frightened me because sometimes it seemed like it would never stop. Finally she caught her breath. "You are fine the way you are," she whispered. "Just be a good person. I know you will be."

I tried to speak, but my throat and my eyes were too full of something.

It'll all work out...All will be fine.

It didn't matter; she was asleep.

I see now that Ellen is more of a mother than I'm giving her credit for. Not just to Anna, who's calm and perfectly content in her arms now, but to me as well. I wish she would reach across the table, and squeeze my shoulders, just as my mother had done. But how do you ask for that? Wouldn't a mother *know*, without you having to ask?

In bed late that night, there are finally no distractions: home-work and chores done, no Anna to entertain, no father to argue with. It used to be the time when I like to just lie there, listen to the quiet, and think about my life, what it might be like after Fullerton: leaving home, going to college, life somewhere else where I can be *someone* else, and not worry about if we have too many dairy cows or not enough, whether we should plant corn or soybeans, or if we should just chuck everything and start all over.

But lately all of that doesn't seem important, not anymore. When I get under the covers, it's only Andy that I think about. I start the day with him, at school, and end it with him, here. Before I know it I'm off and running. I don't need the catalog man anymore, now that I have something real. The problem is that the quiet of the house cuts both ways, and when I get to the end I sometimes clench my jaw so tight that I have a headache for an hour afterward. It makes me wonder how, if you were actually with a real person, someone that you wanted to be with and cared for, how you could possibly not make any sound at all.

And, most important of all, what it would be like with Andy, and how I would keep everything inside, not cry out.

Andy. In the shower room that first day, wet and soapy and grinning at me.

What would happen if I told him the truth?

I thought about you the whole time I was doing it.

I don't want your stupid paper girl with the big boobs.

You're not fooling me. You're not fooling anyone.

After I'm done, I fall asleep right away and have a crazy dream about cows showing up in earth science class, Cathy Martin posing for pictures in our barn, my mother wandering around Fullerton looking for Rebecca. It's one of those dreams where I can see everybody and everything, like I'm hovering above it all, like I'm...*omniscient.* I'm even saying the word in the dream, over and over, though I'm not sure where I've gotten it from. English class with Miss Brintnall? Church? But the problem is, I can't do anything about it: my mother calling out in that singsongy way she had when she was with the cows for Rebecca to come to her, the cows knocking down tables, Cathy taking her clothes off and having to sit on a hay bale while a photographer zooms in on her.

And then Andy shows up at the end. He's lost, too, and just when I think I've found him, or he's found me, he disappears again.

When I wake up, I touch my face. My cheeks are wet, and I wonder if I've made a sound.

9

MORE THAN A FEELING

"Geometry, Spanish, history," Andy snorts. "Who needs this shit?" He spins his *¡En español!* textbook like a Frisbee across the room until it hits the wall with a thud.

You do, if you ever want to make it out of the tenth grade. But of course I just nod, agreeing with everything Andy says. It's become a bad habit, like smoking or an unhealthy food you can't give up. But I can't help myself. Because if it makes Andy smile, a smile that says *Yes, it's you and me, we're in something together,* then it's worth it.

It's Sunday afternoon, with only two weeks to go until Thanksgiving recess, and I've gotten permission to spend it with Andy so we can study our Spanish together. Except for school, Andy's been grounded for the last month because of his bad midterm grades.

Even though the whole point was to study together, and therefore do better in school, my father wasn't crazy about me spending any more time with Andy than I already was. "I think it might be a good idea for you to expand your friendship circle a little bit," he said one cold morning when we were out doing chores, not long after Andy's last visit at our place to work on geometry. "Aren't there other guys you might want to do things with?"

Don't get worked up, I thought as I kept my head down and shoveled more feed for the cows. *Play it cool.*

"It's just not...healthy to spend all your time with one friend. Why not broaden your horizons a bit?"

"Okay," I said, trying to sound noncommittal. I wasn't about to give up Andy. And just as I'd hoped, after some additional bullshitting about how tutoring would be good for me too, since by having to explain it to someone else I'd do better, my father didn't bring it up again. That was a little risky, since he'd been a teacher himself before we started farming and he could have easily seen that I had no clue what I was talking about. But then again maybe he knew it was a lost cause.

"What are you doing for Thanksgiving?" I ask Andy now. Given Andy's short attention span, I've learned that it works best to ease slowly into tutoring: a little bit of small talk first, then on to "Basic Conversations."

Andy shrugs. "The usual shit. We'll eat a lot, and then I'll goof around with my cousins. Last year my uncle let me have a couple beers. He poured it into an empty pop can and so my dad didn't even know."

"What happened after that?"

"I got tired, and then I had to pee really bad," Andy says. "That was about it. You need to have a lot before you feel anything. My uncle and dad usually have to drink a whole twelve pack before anything happens to them."

"So what do they do after that?"

"Not much. Act stupid, mostly, and be loud. The more they drink, the louder they get. My dad yells at my mom for no reason. Or at me. Sometimes that's kind of funny. But it's not like he's ever hit her, or anything. Or me. Sometimes drunk people do that, but he never has. If he ever took a swing at me, I'd give him a couple of these." Andy gets up from the floor and dances from side to side, like a boxer, occasionally throwing a punch, but after about thirty seconds he gets tired and sits back down on the floor. "So what are you going to do?"

"We'll be at my great-aunt Magda's in Mankato—me, my little sister, my dad, and Miss Nesbit."

"Who's Miss Nesbit?"

"She lives with my aunt."

My great-aunt Magda, my grandmother's sister on my mother's side, has never been married. She's lived with Rosemary Nesbit for over thirty years. Miss Nesbit, as I had been taught to call her (to call her "Rosemary" would not have been polite, my mother told me, no matter how long they had lived together and how well we knew her), taught civics and retired the same year Aunt Magda did from her job as a world history teacher at the same high school. Every year, for as long as I can remember, we've spent Thanksgiving at their house.

They're a couple. A *couple* couple.

When I was nine my mother sat me down and explained it all to me: how they loved each other in the same way that a man and a woman could love each other, and that was fine, people could love whomever they wanted and it wasn't up to us to judge. But she didn't have to tell me anything, because I had already figured it out way before that. You could tell it by the way they were with each other. It was hard to explain.

"What does your aunt's friend look like? Is she a fox?"

"What do you mean, a 'fox'?"

Andy's lying on the floor, hands behind his head, then he gets up and paces around the room, restless. "You don't know what a fox is? Paulsen, you are so out of it. That's what my cousin Ted calls a good-looking girl."

I laugh. "She's seventy-four years old."

"So...are they like lezzies or something?"

"Lezzies?" I know what Andy's talking about. I'm just trying to buy some time to figure out what I'm going to say.

"You know, like...girlfriends."

"Yup."

Maybe I shouldn't have said it, because it is Aunt Magda and Miss Nesbit's business. And the last thing I want is Andy telling his mother, who would not only blab it to somebody else but would also try to save them, and before you know it the whole town would be talking about poor dead Vandy Paulsen's aunt from Mankato who is, well, you know. *A little strange.*

But it's a test. I want to see what Andy says, how he responds. If he says "gross," well, I'll know. I'll know what I might be up against.

"Well, I suppose that's cool," Andy says.

"Cool? As in okay?"

"Sure, why not? There's lots of gay people in Minneapolis. I mean, it's not like I knew any when we lived there, but they're there."

"I know. I've read about it in the paper." *And I want to be one someday.*

"It must be weird for your aunt and her friend to live out here in the middle of nowhere Minnesota, with no other lezzies around."

"Maybe. But they've always seemed to like it in Mankato. What about two guys?"

Andy frowns. "Two guys?"

"To be a couple, I mean."

"Hm. I'd have to think about that one." Andy tries to balance his pencil, sharpened end down, on the tip of his finger, then on the tip of his nose. It leaves a smudge that I want to reach out and wipe away, but I don't. "I guess you just have to live and let live. That's what my mom always says when my dad cuts down Black people."

"So if two guys were a couple, it wouldn't bother you?"

"We'd better get back to work," Andy says. He picks up the book he'd thrown and hands it to me. "I gotta turn things around in Spanish. Otherwise I can forget about ever getting my license."

He didn't say, *No, it wouldn't bother me, because I'm madly in love with you and only you.* On the other hand, he didn't say, *God, yes, the very thought makes me want to puke.*

I'm willing to take whatever I can get.

We sit on the floor next to each other, our backs against Andy's bed. As usually happens when we try to study together, Andy lasts about five minutes before he's looking for some other distraction: doodling, launching paper airplanes, studying his fingernails (the "boy" way, of course—like you're looking at your fist, the palm side up—and not the "girl" way—holding your hand out in front of you and spreading your fingers. Something else I learned from Andy). He gets up and paces from the window to the door, then back again.

"Have you ever gotten high?"

Andy knows that I haven't. But it's probably the easiest way for him to bring the subject up. "Have you?"

"A few times. With my sister. She had some. Man, it was great. We went out to the barn and did it."

"So where'd she get it?"

"Her boyfriend. He...deals it. Don't tell anybody I told you."

"I won't."

"Promise?"

"I promise. Cross my heart and..." And then I stop. That's what kids say. *Grow up*, I think. *Be a man.*

"He said he'd sell some to me, but I don't have any money. She let me have some of hers."

"Just because?"

"Well, she can be nice when she wants to be, believe it or not. I think she just asked me because she's afraid to be in the barn by herself at night and she really wanted to get high."

"What was it like?"

Andy slowly closes his eyes until they're little slits. "Man, it's great. I mean, you still know what you're doing and everything, but it's like you're just...a little bit off. In a good way, though. You sort of don't care about anything. You can just feel a lot of...things."

"What kinds of things?"

Andy opens his eyes, looking a little annoyed at my questions. "Well, like music. It just sounds better." He sways a little bit and hums. "Like you can hear things that you'd miss if you weren't high. It's like...*everything's* better. You sort of have to be there. If you've never been high, then you wouldn't really—"

"I know. I wouldn't get it." Suddenly I'm angry, but angry with myself, mostly, for not being...*with it*. But of course it's mainly Andy I'm angry with, for not including me in the first place. For not believing that I *could* be with it, if he'd just give me half a chance.

I try to go back to Spanish, but I can't concentrate. Andy starts singing "More Than a Feeling," a song from the 1970s that he's become completely and totally obsessed with. It's by Boston—that was the name of the group, not the city, he told me. His uncle, who once saw them in a concert, bought the CD for him at a secondhand record store. Andy loved the picture on the CD cover almost as much as the album itself because from one angle it looked like a guitar on fire, but when you turned it around, it was a spaceship. "That is so cool," he said the first time he showed it to me, flipping the jacket over and over. "Isn't that cool?"

"Sort of like an optical illusion," I said.

"Yeah," Andy said. "It's a delusion, all right."

After that Andy played the album every chance he got, both at his house (so loud it made my head pound, and when I got home I had to take a couple of aspirin) and at mine too (much softer after my father knocked on the door and told us to keep it down, because the floor was vibrating and Anna was trying to nap). Andy, with his short attention span, quickly got tired of most of the songs, but not "More Than a Feeling." I helped him write down the lyrics so he could sing along with it, and after a while he had them memorized. I could hear my father's voice in my head: *You know, if that kid put half as much time into his homework as he did learning that song, he'd be a lot better off.* That was probably true, of course. But it didn't matter to me. I felt like the song belonged to both of us. And when he sang it, he was singing it only for me. I didn't have to share it—or him—with anyone. Like something out of a sappy movie, I know, but I couldn't help it.

Andy's trying to distract me now, playing air guitar and swiveling his hips as he sings, full and confident, even if it's slightly off-key, almost matching the high, throbbing voice of the lead singer. On his fourth time through, he pulls off his T-shirt, twirls it around a few times over his head, and throws it on the floor, like he's doing a striptease, though he'd say he's a rocker, not some stripper. That would be too gay. He dances over to his dresser, opens the top drawer, and tosses something to me. It's long and white, like a cigarette, but a lot rounder.

"Do you want to?" he asks.

"Where'd you get this?"

"I just told you. My sister."

"I thought you said you didn't have any money."

Andy sits down next to me, his chest and stomach shiny with his sweat, the sour smell of his underarms starting to fill the room. "Okay, okay, I stole it from her," he says. I watch the thin silver chain that he wears around his neck move up and down. "She'll never miss it."

"Maybe we should study for a while and then try it."

"Paulsen, you're hopeless." He grabs me by the back of my neck and shakes me, but not hard, more playful, his hand warm and sticky on my skin. I want him to leave it there, and then lean over, slowly, and kiss me. I close my eyes and picture it. If I think hard enough about it, maybe I can make it happen.

"So, do you want to get high or not?"

10

CLEARING THE AIR

When I open my eyes, Andy's mother is knocking at the door. It's suppertime and that nice Hansen girl is here to take me home. The room is freezing, and I realize that we'd opened the window to try to keep the smell out. Sometime earlier, I don't know exactly when, I'd taken my shirt off too, and now I'm shivering. We're both on the bed and Andy is asleep, his arm stretched across my middle. Even though I don't want to, I think I should probably move it so I can get up and get dressed. Instead, I keep it there for a little bit longer, so I can feel his skin next to mine, the soft hair on his forearm brushing against me.

Mrs. Olnan knocks again, a little harder this time. "Boys?"

"I gotta go," I whisper. "You awake?"

Andy grunts, then turns over and curls up on his side, like a baby. More than anything I want to curl up too, next to him, my arm around his waist. But then the knocking starts up again.

"I'm sleeping," he says, irritated. "Call me later."

"But—"

"You better go."

"I thought my dad was going to pick me up."

At first it seems odd to see Ellen driving the pickup, but I'm not sure if it's because it's just the first time, or if it's because I'm still high, or a combination of both. Since it's the first time, I don't have anything to compare it to. She looks too small in the driver's seat, the steering wheel too big for her to handle. But then again, everything seems out of proportion to me. I actually sort of like it. I try not to smile, but I can't help it. The more I try not to, the more I want to.

"He had a meeting at the bank. Anna's at the neighbor's. What's so funny?"

"Nothing. Isn't it Sunday? Why would he have a meeting today? Weird." I chew on the insides of my cheeks because more than anything in the world I want to laugh, and I know it wouldn't be good if I did.

"Yes, it's Sunday, and no, I don't know what it's about. You'll have to ask him." Her voice has an edge to it, one that I haven't heard before.

"He hates the farm, you know. He's hated it forever. Well, maybe not forever, but…I hate it too. No I don't, it's just that my mom…" I feel like crying, even though I'm still smiling, and I want to laugh more because I can feel two things at once.

Ellen guns the gas pedal a little bit so the engine doesn't die. My father must have told her about that. "You'd better get yourself together. He'll probably be home by the time we get there."

"What do you mean?" Even though I know perfectly well what she means. She knows what I've been up to, at least the getting high part. But I don't care, not really. Instead I'm thinking about what happened, finally, with Andy Olnan.

"So do you want to or not?" Andy asked it a second time.

"I don't know if we, I mean if I should, or not— "

"Suit yourself." He pulled a lighter out of his pocket.

I stood up. "What about your mom and dad? What about the smell?" On top of everything else, the last thing Andy needed was to get caught getting stoned in his room. But worse than that, I'd be caught too. I'd be just as grounded as Andy was, and probably grounded from him.

But then again, maybe they knew, and had given up trying to do anything about it. And more important, maybe this was an opportunity, an opportunity to show Andy that I was cool. It could only make us closer. He was offering me a chance to be somebody else, somebody that he might want to be with as much as I wanted to be with him, and I figured I'd better take it.

"So?" Andy shrugged. "We'll crack a window." Then he

started up "More Than a Feeling" again and turned up the volume, as if having it on even louder would cover up what we were about to do.

Andy went first, but in just a few minutes he taught me everything I needed to know about getting high: how to hold a joint without burning your fingers, how to not get too much of your slobber on it, how to inhale and keep it in, down in your lungs, until you think your insides are going to explode before you let it go, because you want to make the most of it.

"See? You're a pro already," Andy said, somehow managing to croak the words out at the same time that he was holding his breath.

"Thanks." I tried to sound nonchalant about it, even though I'd never felt prouder in my life, not when I scored my first A in algebra, or figured out on my own how to drive a tractor. I wanted everyone to know about it, how perfect Carl Paulsen was a natural at getting high. Maybe the school paper could do a story about me.

When the joint was gone, and we were lying on his bed together on top of the covers looking at the ceiling but with a good foot and a half between us, I wanted to tell Andy Olnan how my head felt: light, like it was made of Styrofoam, but not as stiff, maybe more like cotton, but not like the kind my mother would stuff in my ears when I was younger and I had an earache. But what other kind was there? The cotton candy I'd eat at the county fair when I was younger, the way it would sit on your tongue for a few second before dissolving? Nothing would stay fixed in my head for more than a moment or two before floating away.

I didn't want to talk. And Andy apparently didn't either, because he was fast asleep, flat on his black, his arms tucked behind his head. Andy had told me that might happen, and that sometimes the best way to end a really good high was to just go to sleep. But wasn't something else supposed to happen first? Weren't we supposed to be, well, high? Act crazy? Do and say crazy things? Or sneak downstairs and wolf down box after box of macaroni and cheese that Andy's mother was sure to have stocked in the kitchen pantry, even though we'd have to figure out how to make it first? Or was the act of smoking a joint enough? My eyes felt heavy, like they were too big for their sockets. Like Andy's must have felt. But I didn't want to sleep, because when I woke up, this would all be over, and I would have missed it.

I turned on my side to watch Andy's stomach go up and down, imagining my index finger tracing a straight line from his throat to his belt buckle, wondering if it would tickle against his bare, damp skin. Would he wake up and be furious, no different than what would happen than if I'd tried it on Kent Neustad? Or would he pretend he was asleep while secretly enjoying it? Or would he wake up, happy that one of us had finally made a move and we could be off and running?

It was time. To *do* something. Fortunately I was just high enough that I felt like I had nothing to lose, but not too high that I wouldn't remember it.

I started with my finger, so lightly that I was mostly tracing air rather than skin, but then I got bolder and went with two fingers, then three, then my whole hand, down and back up again.

And then a little bit of a smile, him breathing a little deeper, eyes still closed.

His lips tasted like the marijuana: smoky and a little sweet. Or maybe mine tasted that way, too, and it was just the two of us together. But I tasted something, and that told me that I must have been doing something right even though I'd never kissed anyone like that before, not for real, and of course not another boy.

But there was something else even more important. He was doing it back. It wasn't just me. Andy was doing it too, even though his eyes stayed closed, which was the way people seemed to do it in the movies. But I kept mine open, because I didn't want to miss anything.

And then there was more pot, more laughing, more kissing, and Andy pulling up my shirt and then over my head, his hands on me just as much as mine were on him. When it was over, we were back on the bed again, our shirts still off but our pants back on, his arm across me. I wasn't sure how it got there, but I hoped that it was because he was holding me, or at least trying to.

"Are you listening to me?"
"What?"
"Out of the truck."
"What for? We're not home yet."
"You heard me."

I close my eyes and put my head down. All of the sudden I have a headache, a bad one, unlike any headache I've ever had before. It's like I need to hold my head in both of my hands, because if I don't, it feels like it will explode, and all of what I remember about what had happened with Andy Olnan will disappear forever. So I hold on even tighter, thinking that if I do it hard enough I can keep it all in somehow, what it felt like, what *he* felt like.

When I look up I see Ellen on the other side of the truck, looking at me through the passenger window. "Get out!" she says again, only this time it's more like yelling, and when I don't she's opening the door and pulling me out. For a second I wonder if we're going to look at cornfields, and I'm back to September, before I really knew Andy, my father wanting me to see something, him trying to tell me something that I can't quite remember now about making money, or not making money. But there's not much to see now, except the dirt and the leftover brown stalks of corn, now flat, and a little bit of snow in between the rows.

"What are you doing?"

"Airing you out," she says. "Walk around. Take some deep breaths. Get your shit together."

"I didn't do anything," I say. "I don't know why you're so mad."

"You're stoned. That's why." She shakes her head and laughs, but it's not a *this is funny* sort of laugh; it's more like a

I'm so disappointed in you laugh, the kind a mother would use to shame her child for doing something wrong. The only other mother-child shaming thing left for her to do is say how disappointed she is in me, and when I say *I'm sorry*, she can say *Well, I'm sorry too*. After all this time, she's finally doing what I kept waiting for her to do: act like a mother, though a very pissed off one.

"What's it to you?"

Ellen looks down, then up at me, her gaze steady. "We think—I mean your dad thinks—you should—"

"Yes, I know. 'Expand my horizons.' He and I had that talk already. And what's with the 'we'? You're not my mother."

There it is. In all the time Ellen has been with us, I've never once used that on her because she's never even tried in the first place. Yes, she did motherly things, but she was there for Anna more than for me. But here I am, using it. And even though I'm stoned I know why. She's trying to make Andy look bad, and I'm trying to get back at her. To hurt her.

But if she's bothered by it, she doesn't let on. "Yes, I know that. And you'd better thank God for that, because if I was, you'd be grounded for the rest of your life, or at least until you left for college."

"My mother would never do that. She'd try to understand what it's like."

Ellen chuckles and shakes her head. "What it's like to do drugs and get caught and then whine about it? Boy, you sure did have an understanding mother."

"She was the best." I can feel tears starting behind my eyes, but I push them back.

"Okay, okay." Ellen holds up her hand. "Truce. This isn't getting us anywhere. For now let's just focus on getting you home. Do you think you're sufficiently sobered up to face your dad?"

"I guess so. So you're not going to say anything?"

"Nope. But if he senses something's up, then you're on your own."

"Thanks. And I'm sorry about, well, you know. This. I didn't mean to—"

Ellen doesn't say anything. Instead she bends towards me and smells my jacket. "Hm. Better. But still not great. Not that your father will notice anyway." Then she gently pries open my right eye and looks at it for what seems like a long time. It starts to water from not being able to blink. "Still pretty red, but I think it'll be okay. I wouldn't spend too much time standing around shooting the breeze with him. Just say you've got a lot of homework to do or something."

"What did you mean about my father, not noticing?"

"That's between you and him. And for Pete's sake, whatever you do, wait until tomorrow to ask him about it."

I have no idea what she means, but I don't want to know. Whatever it was, it can wait. Forever, for all I cared. Nothing else mattered except Andy and what we'd done. And that Ellen wasn't going to tell my father what I'd done.

"You know, Andy likes you." It's out of my mouth before I even think about it.

"What do you mean?"

"He *likes* likes you."

"Well, that's nice, but— "

"He talks about you a lot, ever since he came for supper. He even has a picture of you. I mean, it's not really you but it…sort of looks like you." I leave out the part that I actually have the picture. Things are complicated enough as it is.

"Well, that's sweet and also a bit on the creepy side, but I'm little old for him, don't you think?" For the first time since she picked me up, she smiles a little.

"I know, but it's just that— "

"What?"

"I like him. But I'm not sure about him. If he…is the same way. I'm afraid that he might not be, even though…" But that's as far as I can go.

"I see."

And finally, someone knows.

And more tears, just on the edges. Ellen moves toward me,

like she might be about to hug me, which is something she's never come close to doing before, but then she stops. "We better get home. Your father's going to wonder what happened to us."

But my father, it seems, is out somewhere, our worry about whether he'd figure out what I'd be doing all for nothing. After chores, which I can still do just fine by myself despite still being a little high, the three of us—Ellen, Anna, and me—sit down for our usual Sunday night supper of leftovers from the past week. Andy had said that I might be hungry after getting high (getting the "munchies," he called it), and I was. I ask for seconds, and then thirds, of everything.

"So much for having leftovers of the leftovers," I say. Then I smile at her, hoping she'll smile back, so I can know that everything is okay, and maybe we can even talk about what I told her. Instead she looks away, busies herself wiping Anna's sticky face and hands.

Unfortunately it's Joni Olnan who picks up the phone, but at least she's halfway polite about it this time. "Let me get him," she says. "He might be asleep."

Asleep? I wonder if the pot has hit him, a pro at getting high compared to me, especially hard.

And if he remembers what I did. Or what *we* did. It was both of us. I know that. And if he wants it to happen again as much as I do.

I wait for what seems like a long time, listening to the TV in the background blaring a football game. "Hello?" I finally say. "Anybody there?"

Eventually somebody picks up the phone. Joni again. "He says he's sleeping."

I consider pointing out how that wasn't logically possible— you can't be awake and say that you're sleeping—but given that I want to minimize the time I have to spend with Joni on the telephone I decide not to. "Um, could you please ask him again? It's kind of important." I'm not sure why, but I need to hear his voice, and know that things are okay. I can't wait until tomorrow.

Joni lets out an exasperated sigh and puts the phone down. Another wait, more listening to television commercials.

"What?" It's Andy. Finally.

"Hi there," I say. I try to sound casual, upbeat, but in just two words my voice is already shaky.

"I was sleeping."

"I know. I'm sorry to wake you, but I just wanted to make sure that you were okay about everything, and—"

"I'm fine. Look, I still got homework. I'll see you in school tomorrow."

"But I just wanted—"

I want to make sure that you were okay with what we did.

He hangs up before I can finish. Or even start.

11

SOMEBODY MIGHT HEAR

The next morning, when I see Andy in first period Spanish, I know something's up. Because he's late (his mother probably dropped him off on her way to work), we're not able to talk, and part of me wonders, given how he acted on the phone last night, if he's planned it that way. He's trying to avoid me, or at least put off talking to me for as long as he can. I try a small wave and nod, but I don't get much in return: a quick glance, and then he's back to talking with Dave Miller, a jock who's already playing on the varsity football team and because of that is one of the popular guys. He and Andy act like they've been best friends for years. They're laughing about something, and then pointing, and of course I wonder if it's about me: *Paulsen really is a fag. We got high and he made a move on me...it was gross. I should have decked him, but man, I was too out of it.*

I look at Andy again, trying to catch his eye, but he turns away from me, still huddled with Dave.

Then it's Señorita Johnson clapping her hands, saying buenos días, get your books out.

And from there the day rolls on, a usual Monday, everyone a little groggy and cranky, but following the routine.

Finally it's gym class, which I dread as usual because of Kent Neustad. Today, though, I'm lucky on two counts: Kent is mercifully absent and Dave Miller, Andy's shield, is excused from gym because of the football team. Apparently school officials think he already gets enough exercise. Because I don't have either Kent or Dave to worry about, I have time to think about Andy who's still not talking to me. Instead he makes sure that he's either two people behind or two people ahead of me in the free throw shooting line, and when it's time to run he does sprints to avoid contact with anyone else, including me, until Mr. Todd blows his whistle and yells "Olnan, take it down a notch. This isn't the summer Olympics."

In the locker room I make sure I finish dressing first and I wait outside, at the same place where he waited for me once, a long time ago, it seems, though it hasn't even been three months.

Andy sees me waiting, and stops for a second to look at me, then tries to brush past me. But I put myself in front of him, blocking the way. He looks for a moment like he's going to try push me away, but then he stops.

"Okay, okay," he says. "What do you want?"

"I just want to talk to you for a second."

Andy stands there, his arms folded. "Well?"

"We need to talk about what happened yesterday."

"What happened?"

"You know."

He looks at the floor. "We got high. That was it. What's the big deal?"

"Then why have you been ignoring me all day?"

He still can't look at me. "I…just have a lot of stuff on my mind. That's all. I was going to call you tonight, really I was…"

"You know what happened," I say, trying to keep my voice even, strong. "What I did. And what you did."

Andy shakes his head. "I didn't do anything. You're the one…you did it first," he stammers. "You…"

"I what? I was there. We…kissed, and then we kept going. You didn't want to stop."

"Shut up," he hisses. "Somebody'll hear you." Andy starts to walk away. I follow him.

"You know what happened," I call after him. "You *know*. You and me. We're the same."

He stops and turns around. "Not in a million years, Paulsen. I'm not like you. I'm not a…*faggot* like you. I'm not going to hell. I've been saved."

"What do you mean *saved*? From what?"

Andy ignores the question. "Try doing it with a girl for once.

How about your maid? Maybe you'd get normal." And then he keeps walking.

Unfortunately, as if the day couldn't get any longer, there's still Osterman's class to get through. I'd like nothing more than to skip it, but then Osterman would report me to the principal's office, my father would be called, and it'd turn into a big crisis: *Carl, what in heaven's name is the matter with you? This isn't like you! I'll let it go this time, but...*

I make it just under the wire and only have thirty seconds or so to look around, check the atmosphere of the room, to anticipate what I'm going to have to get through in the next sixty minutes.

There's Dave Miller, playing with a big rubber band (a sling-shot for spit balls, probably, even though we're way too old for that sort of thing. But when you're already on varsity, well, you can do pretty much whatever you want). And Kent Neustad's made it, too, though he's too busy measuring his left bicep with his index finger and thumb to see if it's gotten any bigger since yesterday to pay any attention to anything Osterman is saying, or thank God, to me.

But there's no Andy. On the one hand for him to miss class is not big news. He's done it a bunch of times before, because he couldn't care less about this class or any other one, for that matter. *If I want to skip out, that's my beeswax.* But of course I wonder what our conversation—no, our fight, really—had to do with it. I'm relieved he's not here. Having to see him now, even after what he said, and the way we left things, would hurt too much, like someone with pointy boots kicking you in the stomach.

The ten-minute recap from last week, and then the endless instructions for today's experiment, go over me and disappear into the air. I'm sitting very still, still trying to gauge something like radio waves, or wind, maybe. Or temperature. Anything that will tell me if people know anything about me, about me and Andy. I *do* care what people think about me, after telling

myself for so long that I didn't. And though I don't even know
for sure that anyone is talking about me, I have a pretty good
idea what it would feel like if they were. *Did you hear about that
fruit Paulsen? He put the moves on Andy Olnan when the poor guy was
stoned and couldn't even fight back. If I was Olnan I'd get a few of the
guys together and teach that fag a lesson. Give him a good swift kick where
it counts, if you know what I mean. Serve him right if it never worked
again.*

"Carl?"

"What?"

"Are you ready to do the lab?"

"Lab?"

"Earth to Carl!" It's Cathy Martin, smiling at me.

"I…I guess I am kind of zoned out," I say. "Sorry. To tell
you the truth, I have no idea what we're supposed to do. Sorry
about that. I was just thinking about other stuff."

"Carl Paulsen caught not paying attention? Stop the presses!
Let's get it into the school paper." She smiles again. "Don't
worry, I've got it covered."

And of course, Cathy being Cathy, does have it covered and
then some. We've got thirty minutes to do the lab, and we're
done in ten. "You speedy folks, I'd strongly advise you to check
your work before you ask to be assessed," Mr. Osterman warns,
but with Cathy in charge, there's nothing to worry about. He
stops by the table, gives us the full points, and suggests that
we use the rest of the time to get a head start on reading the
next chapter in the textbook. But neither of us can seem to
concentrate, me for obvious reasons, and why Cathy can't, I
have no idea. She's always seemed like the kind of person who
could concentrate through a tornado, but she seems almost as
distracted as I am. And of course that worries me, because it
must mean she's heard about Andy and me, and maybe the very
thought of having to sit next to me, a…faggot, is more than
she can stand. She was only nice to me during the lab to get it
done so she could get her usual A, and, unfortunately, she had
to take me, the class faggot, along for the ride.

Faggot. Around the time that I was looking up words like "gay" and "homosexual" I had to look up that one too. One of the definitions—a tied up stack of wood, I think it said, wasn't very helpful, and the other one wasn't something that I really wanted to know about: *Disparaging and offensive. A male homosexual.* But once I learned about it, I hoped that maybe I might be lucky and be able to go through life without being called that word.

But when it happened, I thought I could learn to live with Kent Neustad calling me a faggot, at least until gym class was over at the end of tenth grade, when he'd have fewer opportunities.

But to have Andy do the same thing. I'm not quite sure how I am ever going to understand it. Or maybe the problem is that I understand it too well. He is blaming me for something he can't understand about himself, something he can't face. That doesn't make it right.

And there probably isn't a single thing that I can do about it.

"Carl? Is something wrong?"

"Um, no, why?"

"Well, you looked like you just lost your best friend."

I suppose you could say that. I realize then how I must look to her, my head in my hands. Pathetic. "I just have a lot on my mind, that's all. Homework, that sort of stuff. You know." *Including how I actually did it with Andy Olnan, realizing my life's dream, and now he's acting liking I'm dead.* Wouldn't that knock her socks off, as my father would say, cliché hating as he is.

"Andy isn't in class today. Is he sick or something?"

I shrug my shoulders. "Don't know."

"I could have sworn I saw him in first-hour Spanish."

"You did. He's just skipping this class."

"Oh." She puts down the pencil she's been playing with. "You guys are still pretty good friends, aren't you?"

"Andy and me? Oh, sure," I say, trying to sound convincing. I can't tell if she's heard something and is fishing for information, or if she's just trying to make conversation. She's not the type to gossip and spread rumors, and even if she was she would only do it in the nicest possible way. "Sometimes he just does stuff. He doesn't always tell me what his plans are. You know Andy. He's not what you call a stellar student, so for him to skip out isn't that surprising."

"Well, yes, but…"

I look at her, waiting for more.

"It's just that if he skips, that's not going to help him, is it?" She shakes her head. "I don't know why I'm so worried about it."

"You're a good worrier," I say, and for some reason that strikes us both as funny. It feels good to laugh, even just a little bit, given the way the day has unfolded. And laughing makes me think about how much I like Cathy. There's nothing earth shattering about that, but suddenly I'm glad she's sitting next to me. And right now I'm not exactly swamped in the friend department.

"I've been wanting to ask you something. I hope it isn't too out of left field."

Here it comes. The one consolation: since it's Cathy, she'll at least be diplomatic about it. "What?"

"Do you want to get together and do something sometime?"

"You mean you and me?" I've just been asked out by a girl. On a date. Me, Carl Paulsen, who only likes boys. I wonder if it's some sort of joke that she's playing, but again, that's not her style. But still, the timing is, well, odd.

Cathy laughs. "Unless you want to invite someone else along."

"No, not really."

"I mean, just as a friend thing. Not that I wouldn't want to have it be a date, but—"

So not a date after all. Definitely not my day, it seems. Is it possible to still feel rejected even when you're not really interested? But again, a friend is a friend. "No worries, I get it. Sure, why not?"

"We could sort of…talk about things. School. Whatever else you wanted. You know."

I don't know, but again, I can't think of a reason not to.

Maybe she'd have some advice about Andy, though that would mean telling her the whole story. I'm not sure if I'm ready for that.

"When?"

"How about Friday night?"

"Sure."

And before I have time to really think about what's just happened, Mr. Osterman says, "Class dismissed!" in that annoying, military send off way that he has.

Friday night. Cathy Martin. A not-date date. Another first. I can hear my father if I tried to explain that to him: *If you're not interested, be sure to let her down easy.* Then again, he'd probably not even hear that part and be thrilled. *Hallelujah! My only son is straight after all. There is a God.*

And Ellen, who knows the real story, would probably wish I'd just kept it to myself.

And my father's the one who's going to have to be let down easy.

Someday.

On the school bus, there's no Andy. I'm not surprised. But I have to wonder how long he'll be able to keep this up. What lengths will he go just to avoid me? If his mom isn't available to bring him to and from school, what then? A chauffeured limousine? Or maybe he'll just stay home forever, become a high school dropout, just to avoid having to be around me.

It's hard for me to think about being a person someone else wants to avoid. That's never happened to me before. And all because of something I did, something that maybe I shouldn't have done, and that's too late to undo now. I'm going to have to live with it, just as I'm going to have to find a way to live with Andy calling me a faggot.

But as I watch out the window at the brown fields going by, I think about two things. First, I try not to regret what I did. What *we* did. Yes, I admit I maybe was under the influence. But I knew what I was doing. Second, I'm going to try very hard to forgive Andy. Maybe he doesn't…*know* yet. And that's not his fault. It's just not his…time yet. To know who he is. And who knows, maybe someday Andy will probably be asking me to forgive him. And if he did, what would I say?

Yes. You are forgiven. Now we can move on to being together.

I'm going to hold on to that thought for as long as I can.

After being AWOL for what seems like a week, my father has finally reappeared. It's not like he's *really* disappeared. Maybe it's me who's been somewhere else this entire fall, doing chores and schoolwork but not really thinking about them much, not being much of a brother to Anna, or, I suppose, not much of a son. I realize now that most everything has been about Andy: seeing him, talking to him, all leading up to yesterday, which now seems like ages ago.

On my way to do chores I find him working on the lawn mower, even though it's something we're not going to need for another five months. Usually he starts puttering with stuff like that around the beginning of February when he says he needs something to remind him of spring, so he hauls it out and tinkers, even if it's running fine. Why he's suddenly changed the routine, I have no idea. But something's up.

"Hey," he says, not looking up. "I came in here to get something else, saw this, and before I knew it I had the cover off and was testing the spark plugs and one thing led to another. Sometimes you just have to be spontaneous, you know? Do something just for the heck of it, even if doesn't make sense."

"I suppose so." This seems to be the English teacher father, the dreamy one. Any minute I expect him to start giving a lecture on the poetry of Walt Whitman or something. "Spontaneous" and farming don't go together.

"I've been thinking more about things," he says, as he fiddles with a belt on the motor.

"What things?" Even though I can guess.

"Oh, this and that." He looks up at me. "Can you help me with this?" He's trying to unscrew the blade so he can take it off for sharpening and he needs me to hold the rest of the mower in place. "Get a good grip on it, now." In one quick motion the blade is off. He looks at the edges, holding it up to the light to check for dullness. "Looks like we're going to need a new one of these. No matter what, we're always going to need a mower."

I get the feeling he's avoiding the subject, trying to figure out a way to bring up whatever it is he needs to bring up. "Well, we've got tons of time," I say. "Before we have to mow again, I mean."

"Hm." He puts the blade down and looks at me. "I don't think we can go another year."

"What do you mean?" Even though I know perfectly well what he means.

"I've made up my mind. I think we should sell."

For the second time in one day, another punch in the gut.

"Things aren't any better. In fact, they're getting worse. Milk prices are terrible. We're putting more money in than we're getting out. The bank folks are not happy with us. No more extensions on what we owe. Believe me, I've met with them and pleaded. More than once. That's all there is to it. No big mystery." He wipes his greasy hands on a towel and sits down. "I've thought about us doing other things, but—"

"Crops?" He nods. "Why not?"

"It's too late. If we'd started earlier, if I'd gotten my hand on Reg Davidson's land when I had the chance…" We're back to that again. He shakes his head and sighs. "Too late now."

It's starting to make sense to me now: the trips to the bank, the disappearing to think things over without the rest of us breathing down his neck. I can see that it's all been in the works for a while. And where was I? With Andy, or at least thinking constantly about Andy. Not paying attention, not asking questions. I'm slowly coming back to earth.

"I can handle the milking, I could do it all by myself. You do the other stuff. Or Ellen could help, we could pay her a little bit extra—" I'm trying to sound reasonable, calm, but all I'm thinking about is the cows.

Her cows.

My father puts up his hand. "Carl. I've thought of all of that. Over and over. I've been awake at night trying to find a way. We don't have a choice."

He's made up his mind, and without asking me first. But why would he? I'm a sixteen-year-old kid. Yes, I'm his son, but I'm also the hired help. The person who matters the most isn't here to give her opinion, to tell my father this is crazy, we can find a way, let's go through the book one more time, maybe we've missed something.

"So who's going to buy them?" It's a question I don't want to ask, but I need to know.

"I've been talking to an outfit out of South St. Paul."

"And what will happen to them then?" I need to hear him say it out loud. My mother would be doing the same thing.

My father shrugs his shoulders. "They'll get sold to someone else, someone who wants to add to their herd, or—"

"They get butchered."

"I'm sorry, but yes, maybe. I've been dreading this conversation for weeks now, and I didn't want to say anything until I'd made up my mind. You seemed to be off in some other place, anyway, spending time with that Olnan boy. And that's fine. That's what you're supposed to do. Have friends, have fun, not worry every day of the week about getting home in time to milk. And if we're not on the clock constantly, you'll have even more time to do what you want. Have your own life. Me, too, maybe."

It stings to hear him talk about Andy. And even though it doesn't make sense, I want to blame Andy for everything: not only for hurting me, but also for making me think only about him, when I should have been paying more attention to what was happening right under my own nose. "Andy and I..." I start. "We're..." I can't think of a way to put it. *We're not together anymore?* It makes it sounds like we were dating, which in a way we were, though if Andy were to hear me say that, he'd probably have to slug me. "I don't think we'll be spending so much time together. He's...busier now."

My father smiles. "I knew sooner or later Spud would get that boy to do some chores." Lucky for me my father doesn't ask for more details. Or maybe I'm not so lucky. Because maybe it might have helped to be able to talk to him, though I would have no idea how to explain it, how to help him understand who I am. Could a father comfort a son who's lost a boy in the same way that he'd comfort a boy who'd lost a girl? What would be the difference? Hearts, and the ways they can be broken, are the same for everyone, aren't they?

Maybe he knows and he doesn't care. Or maybe he knows I'm gay and the thought of ever talking about it is too unbearably painful to even think about. Losing a wife, and now losing a farm, was more than enough.

My only son…a homosexual! The shame, the shame. Good thing his mother never lived to see this. Even though, let's be honest, it's all her fault, for keeping him too close to her. But then it's mine too, for letting it happen.

Once, I dug out my father's psychology textbook from college and read all about it in the chapter on sexual deviancy. The book was published in 1948. At first I thought there was maybe something to it, but then I decided that there wasn't. To love someone was to love someone, no matter who the people involved were and no matter what Freud said.

I want him to know me. But not today. For now I had to think about how to keep my father from selling our life. Keep him from selling my mother.

"I know how you feel. But this is for you. For you and Anna. Money for college, money so we can take a vacation, go fishing. Maybe not enough for all of that, but it'd be a start, and I'd get a job doing something else. So we could do the things that normal people do for once. Get away from this prison for a couple of days, instead of being tied to those damn milking machines day in and day out."

I don't think I'd ever seen my father pick up a fishing pole in my whole life, but I don't say anything. Because there's nothing more to say.

I leave my father to the lawn mower to do the chores. As

I'm going through my routine, I don't want to think about how many times I'll have left with them, before they're gone, but of course I do. The cows look at me with their steady brown eyes, their mouths in motion as they chew like it was any other day. But it's not.

I thought I'd be crying about Andy, but instead I'm crying about something completely different.

Tears are tears no matter what.

12

DATE NIGHT

Somehow I've made it through the week, to Friday, and to the date with Cathy. I don't like calling it that, but I'm not sure what else it is. A boy and girl get together and do something: it's a date, no matter what and no matter who does the asking. No matter what the boy's intentions are (or aren't, in my case), or what the girl (Cathy) expects.

To be honest, I haven't really thought about it all that much. My mind's been on Andy (of course), and now the cows. As for Andy, he's back in school, like he should be, and it feels like I'm starting to adjust to seeing him while also knowing that we're not friends anymore. It's like we can both occupy the same universe without it being a big problem, at least for him. I don't know what he's thinking, because I can't ask and he's not saying. But at night, when I'm trying to get to sleep, or when I'm milking, or eating my cereal in the morning, I think about what that conversation might be like:

Me: So are you still mad at about what happened with us?

Andy: No, I'm over it.

Me: That's good. So can we can still be...us (whatever that is)?

Andy: Sure. One other thing, though. Just so you know.

Me: What's that?

Andy: You wanted to do it. I didn't. I didn't know what I was doing, you...

And so there'd be that lie between us. Andy lying about what happened, and me letting him get away with it. So instead of one lie, which would be bad enough, there'd be two.

But it's not like we're completely ignoring each other. It's like we're on "nodding" terms: we "nod" to one another when we're on the bus (from our separate seats, of course), or in class. It usually happens when I catch his eye, or he catches mine. I find myself looking at him, something I still can't help, and he sees me doing it. He doesn't look mad about it, which I guess is a good thing. The nod is like a peace offering, but nothing more.

As for the cows, it seems like my father and I have declared a truce about that too. He hasn't said any more about it, and I haven't asked. He knows how I feel. So we continue on, talk about other things, I do my usual chores as if nothing will change.

I guess I'm just trying not to think too far into the future. Getting through this "date" with Cathy Martin will be enough.

Of course Ellen and my father know all about the date, and if Ellen is confused after what I told her in my pot-induced confession, she doesn't let on. Maybe she doesn't believe it, but more likely, in her usual approach to things, she wants to stay out of it. Not in her job description. Maybe someday we'll talk about it again, but for now it's sitting out there, a secret between us taking up space.

As for my father, he acts as if it's the most normal thing in the world and something I do every day, even though it's not. "Such great people, the Martins," he says when I tell him about it. No advice about dos and don'ts on a date, no suggestions about what to wear. Maybe he knows that it's a non-date date, too, or maybe he's too busy figuring out the rest of our lives to pay attention. I'm just grateful it isn't turning into a bigger deal than it already is.

After I've fussed over my hair and fretted about whether I'm wearing the right shirt (non-date or not, why not look good for it?), it's time to go. Because Cathy lives on the opposite side of the county, and to save everybody a little bit of driving because neither Cathy or I have our licenses yet, we've agreed that we'll meet up at the bowling alley, and then Cathy's father will pick us up and then bring me home. That means I'll probably have to go through the third degree with him on the way home, asking about my "intentions" for his daughter. At least that's what I'm imagining, based on old movies and TV shows about fathers and daughters and young men who show up to take the daughter out on a date. *I have no intentions,* I'd say. *I'm looking for a friend. A best friend. And your daughter seems like the ideal candidate.* Then I picture his face as he tries to figure me out.

It's been a while since my father and I have driven anywhere together in the pickup, and it's the first time we've been alone since the "should we sell the cows" discussion nearly a week ago. We go almost a half a mile before either of us says anything.

"Everything okay at school?" my father asks.

"Fine," I say, but that's all. I'm not about to go into the details.

"You know, I sort of miss your nightly confabs with Andy." My English teacher father and his big words. "Our what?"

"Your phone talks. All this week, after supper, I had this feeling that something was missing. And then on Wednesday, it dawned on me what it was. I had gotten used to it, you talking to someone on the phone, and I missed it. Like background music that you don't really think about, but nice to have on." My father turns and smiles at me. "You know?"

I nod but don't say anything. I really just want to change the subject, but to what I don't know. Back to what to do with the cows? Not such a great option either. But to something, anything, other than Andy Olnan. Maybe to Anna, and how much she's grown, or maybe even this phony date that I'm about to go on.

"You boys have a falling out? Because that can happen sometimes. Friends don't always see eye to eye on everything. Perfectly normal."

"I told you. He's just gotten busier now." I know I'm not being very helpful but *we got high and went all the way and now he wants nothing to do with me* didn't seem like such a good answer.

"Well, that's fine," my father says as he fiddles with the rearview mirror. "Like I said before, it wouldn't hurt you to broaden your horizons. Like what you're doing tonight. Even if it's just as friends."

"Hm." Maybe my father does know more than he lets on.

Neither of us says anything for a while. My father hums a song that I don't know, and then starts singing it softly, almost under his breath.

"Nervous?" he finally asks.

"About what?"

"This," he says, tilting his head in the direction of town.

"Not really," I say. "I think it'll be fun." I'm trying to convince myself more than anything.

My father reaches over and pats my shoulder. "Then don't look so serious. You've got lots of time to figure this stuff out." By *stuff*, I don't know what he means, and for once I wish my father, with his college degree ("with high honors," my mother liked to brag) and who's usually so precise with his wording, would be a little more specific.

"You know, Carl, if there's anything you'd like to say about what we talked about the other day, now's a good time." It's out of the blue, and completely off the subject, but at least he's brought it up, even though in another half mile we'll be in town.

"You know what I want," I say. "To keep doing what we're doing."

"Duly noted."

In another minute we're in front of the bowling alley. I start to open the door, but my father reaches over and holds my arm. "Have fun, and be a gentleman," he says. I wave as he pulls away from the curb.

Inside the bowling alley Cathy's waiting for me in the lobby, by the shoe rental window. When we'd talked mid-week about what to do, she'd suggested bowling because while, she said, she wasn't any good at it, we could still have fun, and maybe we could bowl and then have a pizza or something. The idea of bowling seemed a little hokey and 1950s-ish to me, but I quickly agreed, only because I was glad one of us had made a decision. Now, though, I remember my only previous bowling experience, and how bad I was at it: Scotty Herbert's tenth birthday party. Some of the boys were throwing strikes on their first try, while I could only throw the lightest bowling ball between my legs ("granny style," several of them teased, adding "what a wuss" and "leave it to Paulsen to do it the girl way" just to add some more humiliation). But it's too late to back out now.

"Hey there," Cathy says, smiling. Her teeth are perfectly straight and white, not the result of braces, but good genes or maybe just good luck. I know because I overheard another girl in our class, Becky Wendon, moaning about her latest orthodontist appointment to Cathy, and then her envy at Cathy, who reluctantly admitted she'd never even seen an orthodontist.

She's wearing a pale green turtleneck sweater and grey slacks, which seem to go with my white dress shirt with green stripes and my newest pair of jeans. "You look nice," I say.

"You too," she says.

After that there's a little bit of a pause, but Cathy steps in before it turns into something awkward.

"How about some bowling? I'm pretty terrible, but I'm willing to try if you are."

Cathy is *not* a terrible bowler. She's actually very good at it, just as she seems to be good at everything she does. Every other throw turns into either a strike or a spare, and while I don't know a lot about bowling, it's clear she knows how to rack up a lot of points. Why she feels like she has to underestimate herself, I don't know. But she has a way of doing that. I'd seen it in earth science lab, when we're working on something, and she'll say things like, "I don't really know" (even though she does) and, "I'm not sure if this is right" (even though it always is). If I were smart, athletic, and beautiful, I'd let everyone know about it.

As for me and my bowling, I'm nowhere near as good as Cathy, but I'm not as bad as I thought I would be. It helps that she showed me what to do, how to hold the bowl in front of me, line everything up, coordinate your footwork, and then throw it. I still have my share of gutter balls, but at least I'm not bowling the "granny" way anymore. In fact, I actually start to *like* bowling, just as I liked earth science, all thanks to Cathy. *I'm on a date,* I think to myself. *And I'm having a good time.*

After a couple of hours of bowling we sit down to have a pizza. We haven't really been able to talk much during bowling, other than to say things like "good one," "you almost got them all," and "nice try" (from Cathy to me after one of my many gutter balls). But now we're sitting across from each other, and it's too quiet. Since she's the one who asked me out, I keep waiting for her to get the ball rolling. To give myself something to do so I'm not just staring and waiting, I focus my attention on slicing the pizza, but after a couple of minutes of me trying to cut it with the useless plastic knife and trying think of something to say, Cathy steps in.

"Let me try," she says. She takes the knife from me and in less than thirty seconds she has the pizza cut up in eight identical slices: four for each of us.

"Thanks," I say, taking a slice of the pizza. At least eating, like the bowling, will fill up some more of the time.

"You're welcome."

I wolf down the first slice in three bites. I'm ready for my second slice, but to be polite I wait until she's done with hers first.

"I'm a little curious. I'm sort of wondering why you asked me out. If you don't mind me asking."

She takes a slow slip of her Pepsi, like she's trying to buy time to come up with a good answer. "I just thought it might be fun. Did you talk to Andy about it?"

"Um, no. He doesn't know anything about it. We're sort of…not really talking right now." It feels good to say that to someone, but I'm not sure how much more I want to say, even with Cathy, who seems like someone I could trust. I wish I could let it all go. *Andy and I had sex…my first time. It scared him off, and now we're…not anything.*

"I know. Not that I'm spying on you guys or anything, but I know something's changed. Do you want to talk about it?"

I shake my head, even though I really do. "This is kind of important. Big. I mean, I just really need to…"

Cathy puts down her pizza and leans forward. "What is it?"

It all comes out in a rush, like I can't control it. I tell her about me, about what I felt the first time I saw Andy, getting high, about Andy not wanting anything to do with me now, even though I was sure he felt the same thing. When I'm finally done I look down at my half-eaten piece of pizza. Whatever appetite I had is gone, and I wonder if I've just made a huge mistake. Too late now.

"Well," Cathy finally says.

"Well, what?"

"That's a lot of…stuff."

Stuff? It's a little disappointing, given how smart Cathy is about everything else, how she usually knows the exact right thing to say. But I'm grateful she's trying.

"I sort of wondered if that's where things were going with you guys."

"So you know about—"

"You?" Cathy smiles. "Not to sound like a know it all, but I was pretty sure you were…gay." It's hard for her to say the word, but once it's out there she seems relieved. "And then Andy comes along, and I saw what you were like when he was around, and what he was like, and I just knew something was probably going to happen." She looks down at her lap, then at me.

"I've known since that first day in earth science, with the whole partner switch thing. The look on your face…" She starts to laugh. "I'm sorry. I don't mean to make fun. But it was like someone had shot your dog or something."

"Was it that obvious? Do you think everybody else knows?"

She shakes her head. "I wouldn't worry about it. I just happen to have superhuman powers of perception when it comes to people." And then she laughs again, waiting for me to join in, but all I can muster is a weak smile.

"That was a joke. I just had a feeling something was going on."

"So you figured it all out."

Cathy takes a slow sip of her soda and takes a deep breath, as if she's getting ready to ask something important. "And you're completely sure that you're...?"

"Gay?"

"Is that what you're supposed to call it? I don't really know what the preferred word is."

I nod. "Well, the other words for it either make it sound like you belong in a mental hospital or they're not very nice. Believe me, I've heard them all."

"Like what? If you don't mind me asking."

"It's not just guys like Kent Neustad and his friends. One time my dad described Mr. Louden, the guy who runs the funeral home, as a 'nice guy but a little light in his loafers.' That was a new one to go along with the usual fag, fairy, queer, the stuff you hear at school. Adults maybe just have a nicer way of saying it. You don't have to live in a big city to know how people talk about it. About you. I...I mean me."

Cathy looks down at her lap and shakes her head. "People aren't always very nice, are they? To you, I mean. Even your own dad. I thought he might be more up on things, being a teacher and all."

"He doesn't know about me. At least I don't think he does. I haven't gotten that far yet, but when I do...well, it'll be something. That's all I can say."

"I don't mean to ask a lot of dumb questions, but are you really sure?"

I nod again. "I don't know how to explain it. I've always felt that way."

"You don't have to say anything if you don't want to," she says. "But what about Andy?"

"I don't know. I don't think he knows. Maybe he is or maybe he isn't. I thought he was. I hoped he was, but..."

"But you just said that you guys...got together."

I shrug my shoulders. "Maybe he was just using me to... experiment. That and we did get pretty high."

"When you say experiment, you mean that you...had sex?"

"Yup." The rest of it all comes out in a tumble again, like I can't stop myself. I wait for Cathy to absorb what I'm telling her, and then look disgusted, or at least a little surprised, but she doesn't move a muscle. I'm starting to feel like a patient in a psychiatrist's office, or worse yet, like a sinner confessing to a priest. Add "good listener" to Cathy Martin's already long list of stellar qualities.

And from there, the ice broken with the subject, we even try to talk a little bit about the other boys at school, who might be gay too. Since everything feels safe and free with her, I go out on a limb.

"Kent Neustad looks at me," I say.

"What?"

"He does this thing where he looks at me, to get me to look at him, and then he'll say I'm looking even though he looked first."

"So Kent Neustad?"

"He keeps talking about how other people are to keep the attention off him," I say, even though I'm not entirely confident in my theory. It's just nice to be able to try it out on someone else. "I think there's a lot of people out there like that."

"Trying to make others feel bad because they can't deal with who they are," she says.

"Exactly. But try telling that to him." The thought of it, telling Kent Neustad that he's gay, for some reason makes both of us laugh, and we can't stop. It's suddenly the funniest thing in the world, even though it really isn't, but I feel like it's helping us, releasing something. For the first time all night my insides are unclenched.

And then, after what seems like hours and hours of talking, we're both quiet. I've made my big announcement, and I'm not sure where we go from here. More than that, I wonder if I'm going to have to go through this same thing with everyone else I might choose to tell about myself. My father, for one, and Ellen—to not just let it go at what I told her after I'd been with Andy and nothing more. *One person at a time*, I think. *Let's not get all carried away.*

"I could see why it would happen with Andy," Cathy says, slowly, as if she's testing out whether it's safe to go back to him. "I hope you don't mind me telling you this, but ever since he first showed up in school, I've sort of had a crush on him myself. I mean who wouldn't?"

I laugh. "You and me, out on a date that really isn't a date, and we end up liking the same person."

"Except that I never got to…be with him." Cathy laughs too, but now there's something in her face that's a little sad.

I at least got to have that one time with Andy, even though it's not going to happen again, and Cathy doesn't get anything except a date with me that really isn't a date but turns out to be me just using her to spill my guts.

And before I have a chance to say thank you for listening, and for letting me tell another person about who I really am, and to tell her that I'm sorry, her father's there, ready to drive me home.

Neither Cathy nor me say very much on the way to our place. It seems like we're all talked out, and besides that, there isn't any way to continue the conversation in front of her father even if we wanted to. What would we say? *So, Cathy, what do you think I should do? Should I try to get back with Andy again, even though he can't stand the sight of me? Or should I just be glad that he just called me a faggot and didn't send Kent Neustad after me? Or maybe you should try. Maybe he really* does *like girls after all, and I'm only kidding myself. There you go, he's yours.* And then we could laugh, because everything's worked out in the end, and Mr. Martin could even join in too, amazed at the complicated lives of teenagers in a small farming community like ours.

And what was Cathy looking for in the first place? To see if Andy is available?

And what if she was? Nothing wrong with that, though maybe he'd just break her heart too. But at least she'd know what she was getting into.

Finally it's Mr. Martin who breaks the silence. "So, Carl, how are things looking at your place?"

He seems like a nice man, quiet with good manners (that's where Cathy probably gets them), but he's probably heard about what my father is thinking about doing with our cows and wants to see if he can get the true story. I can't blame him for that; he's just doing what everybody else does around here.

"Fine, just fine," I say.

"You're still just doing dairy, right? No crops. Not yet, anyway?"

"Uh-huh. Just dairy."

"Tough business," he says. And with that, he lets it go.

And I'm reminded once again about how life can get complicated.

Andy's no longer my friend, or anything else, if he ever was in the first place.

And the person who's turning out to be my best friend likes the person I like (there's Andy again, right in the middle of it).

And if my father has his way, we're no longer dairy farmers.

If life is about change, as my mother always said, then I know I don't want any part of it.

When I get home, everyone's already asleep: a big relief because now I have some time to figure out how I'm going to rehash my date in a way that satisfies everyone's curiosity without having to get into specifics. On the kitchen table there's a note for me:

C –

HOPE YOU HAD FUN WITH CATHY. LOOKING FORWARD TO HEARING ALL ABOUT IT.

YOUR DAD.

P.S.

ANDY O CALLED.

13

Thanks for Calling

I can't stop re-reading the last line of the note.

Not that there's that much to read, but I do anyway. Over and over. Like if I read it enough times, new words that weren't there before will suddenly jump off the page and will miraculously answer all my questions. But all I have are two words—three if the *O* counts.

What does it mean that he called? Called to talk? *Of course to talk, idiot.* But what about? Why now? To say that he is sorry for what he said, to say that he wants to get back together? *Back together.* Back together to do what? Be friends but forget what happened? Or back together to be, well, back together. To be together when we're not stoned, so we can really see each other and know what it means to be with other. Happily ever after. But somehow I have a feeling it's not going to be that easy. That something's about to be broken all over again.

I look at the kitchen clock. 11:15. Too late to do anything about it now. But it's Friday night! Doesn't everybody stay up a little later on Friday nights?

But then I think about the phone ringing at Andy's house, his father rousted out of bed because of some goddamned kid without the common sense to know not to call at that hour. Some kid who just HAS to talk to his no-good son who, come to think of it, won't help around the house, much less the farm. Don't your friends have enough sense not to call in the middle of the night? And then maybe a slap, like the one Andy's mother gave him the first time I was at his house for supper. But since it's his father, it could be something worse, and Andy being Andy, might hit back, or least give him a push, and before you know it they're trading punches, wrestling around on the floor, Andy's mother screaming for them to stop but they just keep going.

And it would be all my fault.

And despite everything, Andy doesn't deserve that.

I brush my teeth, wash my face, do my usual routine, knowing all along that it'll be a while before sleep comes, if it does at all.

So I drag out the catalog from underneath my bed, because sometimes when I can't sleep, just turning the pages, and looking at the same things I've always looked at, even if it's stoves and refrigerators, calms me down. It's something my mother used to do when I was little and I couldn't settle down. She'd put me on her lap, and we'd look at it together, and before long I was out. It still works.

And as I get into bed and settle the catalog in my lap, I realize that it's been a long time since I looked at him: my another. Even though it's completely ridiculous and childish, I feel a little twinge of...what? Guilt? It's like I've been neglectful, and he might feel bad that I haven't been to see him for a while. But he's still there, still smiling, still holding his chin, still thinking about something, even if it's how soon he can relax, put a pair of pants on, get ready for another picture in another outfit, or even in another catalog.

I'd forgotten that I'd put the sketch of Andy next to him, the one I started that day in earth science when Mr. Osterman separated us, as if they could keep each other company. I always thought I might finish it and give it to him for Christmas, but I never got around to it. I start to crumple it up, then stop, not ready to let go, not just yet.

And there's still Ellen, the picture one, the only gift he gave me, stuck there too, waiting for Andy to make up his mind about who he is. She's going to be waiting a long time.

I know now that Andy is probably not going to be my another, any more than the man in his underwear could be. It comes to me slowly, like it's in the corner of my eye and moving, and suddenly, it's there in front of me, and there's nothing to do but face it.

Why I suddenly know it, at midnight on a Friday night in November not long after I've turned sixteen years old, just after I've had my first and probably only date with a girl, I have no idea. But sometimes things choose us, rather than us choosing them. More of my mother's wisdom—that's what she said when I asked her once when I was very little why we lived on a farm and not in town and why my dad didn't have a job in a bank or a factory or a hospital. Like the dads I'd learned about in picture books that she and I read together, over and over.

I want to be able to hope for Andy for just a little while longer. But maybe knowing that I could feel that way about a real person is enough.

Not long after that I fall asleep, and when I wake up the catalog is sitting on my chest, closed.

At breakfast the next morning I go over the whole date with Cathy with my father and Ellen: the bowling, the pizza, everything except the most important part. What would I say? *I told Cathy Martin that I was in love with Andy Olnan and we fooled around, but first I had to get through the part where I told her that I liked boys.*

"So am I right to assume that you're going to ask her out again?" my father asks. Even though he's worded the question like a prosecuting attorney, there's something in his voice, a hopefulness that maybe I've turned out okay after all, that I just needed a little more time. Nothing wrong with a late bloomer, he'd say, so long as you bloom.

"Well, she asked me, remember. But maybe."

Ellen gives me a look.

"But just as friends."

My father frowns. "Oh. Well, nothing wrong with friends."

It doesn't seem right to offer him any encouragement that I'm going to live happily ever after with Cathy Martin, or with any other girl, for that matter. And that I told Ellen before him seems wrong, too, though I told someone. Ellen and Cathy: two down, how many more in my life to go? I know that, sooner or later, the talk with my father is coming. Not specifically about what happened with Andy Olnan, necessarily, but the *truth*.

Or to put it another way, my big *secret*, though I'd rather not think of it that way, because then it sounds like I'm keeping something from him when I'm really not; it's been there all the time. I'm the only one who feels like it's a secret. I think of it as something on my to-do list: get through high school, go to college in the Twin Cities, tell my father that I'm gay. Or, given my father and how he feels about the English language and the importance of always using the right word at the right time, maybe the scientific term—*homosexual*—would be better.

But for today, the goal is to sort things out with Andy, or at least figure out how to say goodbye.

I'm in the living room, the telephone on my lap, and for what feels like the most important conversation of my life, I actually have the whole house to myself. Ellen's taken Anna into town to look for a new pair of winter boots because she's already outgrown the ones we bought for her last year. My father's out fixing the fence on the northern edge of our pasture so the cows don't escape, not that they would anyway; if anything it'd be impossible to get them to leave. And of course that brings up the other dilemma in my life: what our future is, what happens next with the farm. It's been there, on the fringes, trying to find a way in, but I keep pushing it out, locking the door. I have this idea that once I have Andy figured out, and it seems like I do, then I can move on to the next item on the list. *I've got all of this under control*, I think as I dial the number. *I'm strong.*

I'm not ready when it's Andy who answers the phone. I was expecting the usual routine of asking to speak to Andy, please, followed by a little chitchat with his mother about Anna, the weather, safe things, followed by background comments from his sister, who's probably sitting at the kitchen table because she just got out of bed, smoking a cigarette, about Andy's boyfriend being on the phone or some other smart comment. But there he is, and there's nowhere to go except through.

"My dad said you called last night." I think about my tone of voice: all official business, not nasty, but not friendly either. The way my mother would be when she had to call to complain

about Sears sending the wrong-sized dress, or when she wanted
to know from the electric company why they had made a mistake on the bill. *You don't get anywhere being mean,* she'd said when
I asked her once why she didn't sound like herself, *but you can't
let them walk all over you either.* I can't see any reason to be mean
to Andy. There's no way that I could ever be, even though he's
hurt me. But to pretend that everything is fine when it's not
doesn't seem right either. *I'd like the size 6 sent to me immediately.*
There it is: the tone that I want.

"Hey," he says. *Hey.* It's soft, drawn out a little bit, all Andy.
I picture him saying it, with a little half smile, his head cocked
to one side, which makes his hair fall over one eye more than
the other, his arms folded in front. I can feel the hardness in
my throat, in my chest, which I didn't realize was even there,
starting to melt away, warmth spreading from my toes all the
way up into my head.

I think I'm in trouble.

"So how ya' been?" he asks.

"Okay." Maybe if I keep it short, I can get out of this thing
in one piece.

"So," he says. He lets it hang out there for a few seconds. "So
I heard you had a big date last night." He chuckles.

"How'd you hear about that?" Even though I know perfectly
well how. Somebody probably saw us at the bowling alley, or
getting into Cathy's dad's car. Word gets around.

"You. On a date. Man, you surprise me."

Man. The old Andy. I realize how much I'd missed it, how
close he is at this very moment even over the telephone. How
easy it would be for things to go back to the way they were. If
I was just willing to…what? Go along? Forget?

"So spill it, Paulsen. What all did you guys do?"

"Well, it wasn't really a date. It—"

"It sure sounds like a date to me. Then what was it?"

"I don't know." My mother on the phone with her Sears
voice is long gone. "I—I just thought it would be fun to do
something with Cathy Martin."

"Was it?"

Fun really doesn't describe it when you spill your guts to someone about yourself. "We had a nice time," I say.

"Did you get any?"

"Any what?" Even though I know perfectly well what he means.

"You know."

"It wasn't like that. We're just friends. Good friends. She's a good listener."

"Only you would go out on date with a chick and talk." Andy lets out a long sigh. "I was really hoping that maybe you were okay."

"I *am* okay," I say. "I'm pretty good, actually."

"I mean okay as in, well, okay. Not…"

"Gay?"

"Um-hm."

"You can say it. It's not like it's contagious or anything."

"Look." Then another long sigh. "I know I shouldn't have called you what I did. That was bad. But I still want us to hang out. And I just thought that if you were liking girls now, then it would be easier, because that meant you were…okay."

"As in not gay."

"Uh-huh."

"But I am. I've always been. I know that."

More silence, both of us breathing. "If you just hadn't done that…" He stops, then tries again. "If only you weren't, then everything would be…good. With us. Being friends, I mean."

"But I did do it. I did it because I—"

"Jeez, don't say it," he says, his voice suddenly sharp. "Don't even fucking say it."

And so I don't. I don't need to. Because we both know that everything's changed between Andy and me, and for good.

"I can't do it," Andy says. "I'm not like you. I'm not—"

"Ready?"

Andy doesn't answer.

There's nothing left to say. There's just the two of us, and more breathing.

But even at the end, we try to be nice. Not just me. Andy, too. No names, no hanging up on each other.

"See you in school," he says.

"See you," I say. Because I will see him. Every day for the next couple of years.

More change. It's not like my mother hadn't warned me. If I wasn't ready before, I'm ready now.

14

A SECRET LIFE

And I do see him. Every day, several times a day. Gym, English, earth science, the bus. All of our usual places. It's a small town, small school, small everything, so there's no way around it. We're both there, but separate. In our own orbits, as my mother would have said. When she noticed me daydreaming, which I did (and do) often, she'd say, *Carl? Where are you? Have you left our solar system entirely?* And for a few months, at least, I'd been orbiting in the solar system of Andy Olnan. Now I've no one to orbit but myself, which really isn't possible, when you think about it. A planet has to have a moon.

So in that way we seem to have reached a sort of understanding. We have to co-exist somehow, keep the secret of what happened between us. Except, of course, I hadn't; Cathy knows the whole story, and Ellen a part of it, and while Ellen and I have not talked about it since, I am glad about that. It made it real. Whether Andy went and told anybody, I don't know, but I can't imagine that he has. Because then it would have to be real to him too, and he wouldn't want that.

But still, I'm struggling to put a name to what happened with us, because if I can, then maybe I can understand it. We... what? Split up? Could you call it that if you weren't really a couple in the first place? Or maybe it's better to use my father's "on the outs" description, though that makes it seem like we'll eventually be back on the "in" again, which I know isn't likely to happen. But I know that terminology doesn't much matter when it comes to how you feel. You can still miss someone when they're right there in front of you.

A few days after our date, there's another invitation from Cathy.

Only this time it's not to bowl, but to get together at her house after school.

"You can come home with me on the bus, and then my mom will run you home."

"I'll have to get my dad to cover my chores," I say, even though I know my father might be thrilled to know that I am getting together with Cathy again, even if it is just to be friends, and to know that there might still be hope. "But that sounds good. We need to get going on that stupid project for Osterman's class."

"Good. We can work on the project, but there's…something else. It's…sort of awkward to go into all of it on the phone."

My stomach drops to the floor. "You heard something about me at school."

"No, that's not it."

"Andy Olnan, then."

"You're getting warmer, but let's just wait until—"

"Tell me now. Please." There he is, back in my orbit. Again.

"We'll talk."

Just as I figured, my father says, "Go, I'll take care of things, be polite and be sure to wipe your feet and give the Martins my best."

Cathy and I—after small talk on the bus about the project and what we have to do and how we wish Osterman would just slack off a bit on the homework—let ourselves in through the back door to the kitchen, where Cathy's mother is stirring something in a bowl.

"We'll be up in my room," Cathy says. "We're going to work on our earth science project."

Her mother turns to me and smiles. "Nice to see you, Carl. How's everything at your place? Your dad doing okay with everything?"

"He's good." I wonder what the "everything" is that she's talking about, what's been going around town about our maybe selling out. But in true Minnesotan fashion, she wouldn't think of coming right out and asking if we're really thinking of getting out of dairy farming. Too nosy, even though I'm sure she's already heard things and would love to get the true story.

"And your little sister?"

"She's good too."

"That's good. She's a real sweetie. Saw her out with...who's the young lady who helps out at your place?"

"Ellen."

"Oh, that's right. The Hansen girl. She seemed real nice."

"She is."

"Bars will be out of the oven in about twenty minutes. Study hard."

Her mother doesn't say anything about leaving the door open, or why don't you just work down here at the dining room table (so she can keep an eye on things). Maybe she knows, without even being told, that she has nothing to worry about with me. Or maybe she does know; Cathy seems like the kind of daughter that would tell her mother everything, and I didn't exactly swear her to secrecy. And somehow I have a feeling that she would be fine with who I was too. Not just because she is Cathy's mother, and Cathy turned out the way she did because of her. But also because maybe it is easier for someone else's mother to be okay with it, since in the end it is going to be some other parents' problem.

I've never been in a teenage girl's bedroom before, and I feel like a trespasser, like it's some sacred space either reserved only for other teenage girls or a boy all hot to take advantage of the situation. I expect to see a big canopy bed, posters of teen heartthrobs on the walls, and a lot of pink. I probably got that idea from episodes of 70s sitcoms, where I seem to get a lot of my information from. *Girly.* But Cathy's bedroom is well, pretty...minimal. I think that's the right word. Definitely not girly. A single bed, a desk, a white wicker rocking chair with a green cushion, walls painted the same soothing shade of green. Not a princess phone in sight. A shelf full of adult-looking books: no Nancy Drew or Harry Potter or Laura Ingalls Wilder. When I think about it, it fits her perfectly. Straightforward, to the point, no games.

The look on her face now says the same thing. Something is definitely up.

"You should have seen my dad when I asked him if he'd do chores so I could come over. All…hopeful and everything. It was pretty sad, knowing that someday I'm going to have to burst his bubble." I laugh, trying to lighten the mood, but it comes out like a nervous, high-pitched giggle. "You look all serious. What's going on?"

"Well…I might as well just get to it. It's about Andy. Something that I found out."

In her usual matter-of-fact way, and in perfectly constructed sentences and paragraphs, Cathy tells me why exactly Andy Olnan and his family decided to come back to Fullerton.

It has absolutely nothing to do with inheriting his grandmother's land, or Spud Olnan suddenly wanting to be a farmer.

It has everything to do with Andy Olnan.

To save Andy Olnan from the evil temptations of big city life.

Until I messed up the plan.

In a nutshell: handsome fifteen-year-old boy all of a sudden has nice clothes, money, other goodies; parents get suspicious because there is no way all of that could have come from mowing lawns and shoveling sidewalks; parents do some investigating and find out that their boy has been hanging out (and more) with an older guy (okay, just a couple of years older, but they still flip out) when they haven't been paying attention, never mind how they can't have not known what's going on. But apparently they don't. Eventually there's a big blow out, Andy is grounded for life, sent to the local minister to save him from evil.

Except that it doesn't work.

Because it wasn't just about the stuff. Something else was going on. Between them.

Andy wasn't going to let him go. Because he loved him.

Well, I don't know if that last part is true, but according to Cathy, Andy does just about everything he can to keep seeing him: skipping school, sneaking out at night, lying about his whereabouts so they won't find out. But of course eventually they do find out. More trips to the minister and more praying, even the police get involved even though there's not much they can do about it. And so it keeps going.

And so to go through all of that? Andy had to have loved him. I'm sure of it.

And more than that, he had to have loved Andy too.

"Wow." It's about all I can think of to say.

Except there's a couple of missing pieces.

"How did you find all this out?"

"Let's just say I know someone who knows someone at his old school and everybody knew about it. Does it matter?"

"I guess not."

"Maybe I shouldn't have said anything."

"No, I'm glad you did." But maybe I'm not so glad. Because now I know that there was someone else, before. *So what does that make me?*

Of course there's one more piece of the puzzle to fill in, and Cathy's on top of that too. "That's the whole reason they moved here," she says. "My friend—well, her friend who was in the same class as Andy at his old school—said that his parents were at the end of their rope about the whole thing. He was getting into fights with his dad, and finally, after Andy gave him a black eye they were going to send him to some religious school to—"

"Fix him."

Cathy nods.

"But they didn't."

"Nope. Andy's mom begged and pleaded with his dad to not send him away, and so they moved here instead."

"That seems like a lot of work to try to fix something that can't be fixed."

"I know."

"So they pack up everything and move here. No temptation and all that."

"Yup."

"But then he met me."

Cathy sighs but doesn't say anything.

"And so he lied to me. About everything."

"Everything?"

"Well, almost everything. Afterward acted like he didn't know what he was doing, that he'd been saved."

"Maybe he thought he was, and he just had a slip. Sort of like an alcoholic, you know?" Cathy bites her lip. "I'm sorry, I didn't mean it to sound like it's an addiction or something."

"No worries. I know what you mean. To him maybe it was like that, and probably to his parents too." But somehow that doesn't make me feel better. "I just wish he'd had a lapse with someone else." But maybe that wasn't true, either. I'd had an... experience, finally. It is probably just as well to have had it with Andy Olnan as anyone else.

No, that isn't it.

This is it: it was supposed to have been the first time for the both of us. All of a sudden that seems important, that we had shared that. I hadn't realized that until now. We were in the same place, even if Andy didn't want it to be true. But that's a lie now. He was way ahead of me, and with someone else. He will always be ahead of me, whether he wants to admit it or not, and it is probably too late for him to come back and for us to start over.

"I hope I did the right thing by telling you," Cathy says. "Now I'm not so sure."

All I can do is nod. "We should work on our project."

And so we work quietly together, for the next hour, putting colored pins on a map of the world that we've mounted on cardboard to show where the most earthquakes have occurred.

And somehow that seems like the most logical thing to do, to be talking about the shakiness of the world.

15

Tennis, Anyone?

On the way home, I balance a dozen still warm brownies wrapped in aluminum foil on my lap. Cathy's mother insisted—a thank you for coming over and helping Cathy with our project—though I didn't put up much of a fight. Ellen isn't much of a baker, I'm afraid, and with everything she has to do who can blame her. At first I worry that it might be awkward, me bearing baked goods from someone else's mother when, as a mother stand-in of sorts, that's supposed to be her territory. But then I realize that, like most everything else these days, I'm probably overthinking it; she'll probably be glad for a treat for all of us regardless of the source. *Forget about the damn brownies,* I think as the stiff stalks of picked corn speed by, the snow in between already gray even though it's barely December.

After Cathy gave me the big news about Andy Olnan, there wasn't much left to say. True to our word, we did try to work on our project, though our hearts, at least mine, weren't really in it. We'd talk about this point or that point and what to put into the report about how best to explain the history of the Richter scale and how detailed we should get, but then we'd drift back to Andy, me saying something like *unreal* and Cathy agreeing with her own *yes, unreal* but that would be it. And Cathy, excellent teen therapist that she is, occasionally asking if I was okay or wanted to talk about it some more. *No, let's just keep working.* We'd exhausted the subject.

Now, in the car, a few miles from home, I try to summon something like anger, but it isn't there. Perhaps that will come later, but for now I can't keep a picture out of my head: Andy's parents on the one side, hanging and pulling for dear life, the boy—Cathy seemed to know everything but his name—on the other, doing the same, with Andy in the middle. I know it isn't exactly the same, but I remember the story from Sunday school or somewhere about two people wanting the same thing, and the only way they could get it was to destroy the very thing they were fighting for. Thinking about it like that makes it hard to stay mad, though I can find lots of reasons to be.

You're a phony.

All that stuff with the picture and Ellen.

You lied.

You could have told me.

You said you didn't know what was happening, what to do, how it happened, when you knew way better than me all along what to do. You could have shown me.

But then I realize that, lies or not, he taught me a lot.

What your body can feel like, what it can do, when it is with the right person.

Andy is the right person for me. At least for now.

But it isn't going to work the other way around.

I let out a deep sigh, so deep there's a little *aah* to it. Cathy, in the front seat, turns around. "Everything all right back there?"

I nod but don't say anything.

She nods, too, because she knows everything is not all right. But it'll have to be. For now.

I let myself in the kitchen door, ready to present the brownies to Ellen, but she and Anna are nowhere to be found, though I can smell supper in the oven. I look at the clock above the sink: chore time. They're probably out helping my father, who's helping me out so I could go to Cathy's. But then I hear my father's voice on the telephone in the living room.

"Yes, I know it's been a while, but—I mean, I taught for quite a few years, and I was good at it. The whole getting back on the bicycle thing, you know?" He chuckles; it's not a relaxed, we're just having a conversation sort of chuckle, but more strained, like he's trying too hard. Is it possible to get all of that out of a five second chuckle? But I could hear it. Besides that, it surprises me to hear my father using a cliché, because those, like cell phones, are something he couldn't abide. And why shouldn't he be sounding a little desperate?

"Yes, I know it's been a while," he says again. "But, with a little bit of work I know I could—"

He's trying to get a job.

"No, I haven't done anything with it, not lately. I thought about trying to do some subbing, but pretty tough to do when you're running a dairy farm. It takes everything you've got and then some. You know?"

No, they couldn't know, unless they've done it. Yes, it is everything. But we knew that, didn't we, and we wanted it still. She did, at least.

"Moving is definitely not a problem... No, I don't know much about Ely, other than it's a ways up there! Almost to Canada, as I recall... But pretty country. Really nice. I'd think we'd like it... Yes, two. My son just turned sixteen, and then a little girl, about to turn four...yes, that is quite a spread, isn't it! One of life's little surprises, I guess." More laughter. My father telling a stranger that Anna wasn't planned, something he's never even told me.

And then there's Ely. *Ely!* I remember it from a map in sixth-grade geography class, when we were studying Minnesota. Easy to remember: only three letters and a dot all by itself, not many other dots nearby. The water it sits on belongs to both the United States and Canada, Mrs. Gunderson, the teacher, had said. To get anywhere you have to take a canoe, and bring all of your stuff with you, and where there's no water you have to carry everything until you can put it all in the water again and float to the next spot, where you will probably have to do the whole thing all over again. Even farther away than Duluth, where Andy and I said we were going to go someday, to look at the lake. Would there be any Andys in Ely? Could I start all over with that, too, but this time hope for someone who won't lie about who he is?

So unless I'm going to take over at the ripe old age of sixteen and run the place myself, leaving my father free to be an English teacher at the edge of the earth, there's only one explanation. We're selling. He's made up his mind.

Without telling me about it first.

"Well, I've kept up my license, if that's a concern, just because…well you never know how things are going to turn out.
Best to have a backup plan, right? We were going to make a go
of it, because it was my wife's. Her folks', I mean, but then she
inherited it. But after she died, and with how bad things are
with dairy, it's just not, well, I'm afraid my heart's just not in it
anymore."

His heart. But what about mine?

After that, there's more discussion about salaries ("I can live
with it"—in other words it doesn't pay very much, but it's something and certainly better than going broke as a dairy farmer),
the housing market ("Really? Not bad for a three bedroom
house"), even the possibility of my father doing some tennis
coaching ("I'm open to that"), even though he's never picked
up a racket in his life and he despises organized sports almost as
much as he despises clichés and cell phones. And through it all,
there's still that sound of begging in his voice, trying to please
and say the right thing. If I weren't holding on to the plate of
brownies I'd be covering my ears.

"Well, I'm happy to talk to you more about it anytime," my
father says, as the conversation seems to be winding down.
"Anytime," he says again. "I can drive up and we can meet in
person, too…no, I understand you have other people to talk to.
I'll wait to hear back from you then. Thanks so much…bye."

I'm sad, of course, because of what's going to happen next,
but it's just one more to add to the list of other sadnesses, if
that can be a word: the sadness about Andy and the lie that
seems to be his life, the sadness, like it's in my bones, about my
mother, which never goes away, not really.

And now the sadness of hearing my father having to talk
someone into giving him a job because it's the only way he
thinks he can take care of us.

I know I should be angry, but as I stand here, still holding
the brownies, frozen in place, I can't find it. Instead, I want to
go in the living room, let him know I know everything, tell him
it's okay.

But I know I can't, because then he'll know that I know, and that I heard how hard he tried and begged without trying to make it seem like he was begging and a father shouldn't be humiliated in front of his son. Even a father who is about to make a big mistake.

"Carl? Is that you?"

"It's me."

My father comes into the kitchen. "Brownies! That was sweet of them. How did the studying go?"

"It went." *And, oh, I found out that Andy Olnan, my total fixation for the last three months and to whom (who?) I lost my virginity, had a secret boyfriend before me but somehow never got around to telling me that.* Maybe my father can correct the who/whom problem; good practice for his new job. "Ellen and Anna still doing chores?"

"Should be about finished by now. I had some calls to make."

Now's my chance, but I don't take it. A good son, a good man, not only does not embarrass his father, he doesn't eavesdrop, either. Let him tell me when he's ready, and maybe that'll give me more time to come up with ways to talk him out of it.

Or maybe it's a done deal.

"I should go out," I say. "Make sure everything's okay."

"I'm sure they have it under control but I'll go," my father says. "If you want to just relax and wash up."

"No, I'll go. *You* relax. Have a brownie."

And by the time I get out there, my father's right. There's nothing left for me to do. I meet Ellen and Anna coming up the path from the barn. Anna runs over to me and demands to be picked up. Before long she'll be too big for us to carry.

"How was the studying? Still getting smarter?"

Not when it comes to Andy Olnan, I think. "I guess. Cathy's mom sent some brownies for us. They're on the kitchen counter."

"Brownies!" Anna claps her hands, then pats my face as a thank you. I set her down so she can run to the house and have one.

"Well, that was sweet of her."

"I know. They're nice people."

"What's wrong? You seem a little down."

"Nothing. I'm just tired of Mr. Osterman and earth science and sort of everything."

Ellen rolls her eyes. "Osterman. A good case for early retirement for teachers. But I guess he's all right."

"All right, I guess."

"I'd better go in and get that hot dish out before it's burnt to a crisp."

"Andy and I are…not together anymore. Just so you know."

There. Why shouldn't she know, since she knows everything else?

"I figured as much."

"How did you know that?"

She smiles. "It's not that hard. I see a lot of things around here. The problem is, I'm not sure how involved I should be, or if I even want to be. I'm not the mom, I'm not the sister. I'm mostly here for her." She points to Anna, now back outside, on the swing set, her mouth covered in chocolate.

"That day you picked me up from Andy's, I know I was a mess, but I think I just needed to tell somebody. And you just happened to be there."

"Lucky me." Ellen chuckles. "I shouldn't make fun. I'm glad you did, but afterward I didn't know what I should do about it. Again, I'm not—"

"I know. You're not the mom of me." And we both laugh at that, hard, because we both know it's close to the good old "you're not the boss of me" that I sometimes wanted to use with my mother and father but never had the opportunity. It feels good to laugh, like something's being released. But then we stop, and I'm not sure where we go from here. I could tell her about Andy and what I found out, but not now. Someday? Or maybe not.

"Have you talked to your father about it?"

I shake my head. "He has enough on his mind."

"Not so much that he wouldn't be willing to talk about it."

"Maybe soon." *Once we've resettled near the Arctic Circle and we have tons of time to fill because there'll be no more chores, no more cows.*

"I know he's thinking about selling, but you probably know that."

"He's looking for a teaching job. I just heard him talking about it. Way up north."

"And then I'm out of a job, I guess." Ellen laughs again, but it feels more forced this time, to cover up for something else.

I've been so busy thinking about everything else, it hadn't occurred to me what would happen to Ellen if we sold the farm. My father said we'd want a three bedroom house: one for me, one for him, one for Anna. No Ellen. And who'd want to go to the ends of the earth with us anyway?

"What are you going to do next? I mean, after you're done here."

"To be perfectly honest with you, I have no idea," Ellen says. "But I guess I'd figure out something. Move back home with my parents, for a start. Then what? Who knows. School, maybe. Any suggestions?"

Stay with us, I'm thinking, as the three of us walk back to the house together. *When we're stuck out in the wilderness, you can have my room. I'll sleep on the bearskin rug in the living room in front of the fireplace which will be going night and day so we don't freeze to death.*

It's the longest she and I have ever talked, and already I'm missing it.

16

The Real World

When I see Andy Olnan in the halls at school now, just a few weeks until Christmas vacation and near the end of the longest semester of my life, I do what I can to be heading in the other direction. But it's hard to do when you're still a *P* and he's still an *O* and there's nothing you can do about it. There are still lockers and class lists and seating charts where they line you up that way to make life easier even though it's anything but, and it's like we will always be next to one another, at least in name only, until one of us moves away, or changes our name, and neither of those is likely to happen anytime soon. Andy just got here, and if what happened with me is any sign, he's got a long way to go before he's saved and the whole plan will have been a success.

As for where else I might be going, no new developments there. Since I heard my father talking to that person at Ely nothing seems to have changed, no trips up that way planned, as far as I know, and if he is going, it seems like I'd be sure to know about it. Life goes on, with chores and milking and hot dish Monday nights, pot roast on Tuesdays, more hot dish on Wednesdays, chicken on Thursdays, frozen pizza on Fridays, because Ellen visits her folks then, leftovers on the weekend.

And instead of talking to Andy most nights, it's Cathy who's on the phone with me, talking about everything and nothing at the same time. That is, most everything except Andy Olnan, even though we share him more than anything else. But Cathy does offer advice, even if I'm not able to take it: find someone else. Not here, of course, but Minneapolis or even Mankato, the only decent-sized town close by. Keep working on your dad to get you that cell phone, a laptop, so you can get into one of those apps where people meet each other.

I say thank you, I will, but for now he has his hands full. Maybe after we move to Antarctica, but the possibilities there don't seem too promising.

So back in the real world, Andy and I still co-exist, and while each of us has turned avoiding one another into an art form, for me he's always there in some way, even if it's just in my head. At our lockers, we busy ourselves with our books, our jackets, or whatever other nonexistent things we are looking for so we can avoid eye contact. And even when we're not standing there in our stalls, I can still feel him, and if I close my eyes we're back in his room, where he danced and got sweaty and played that stupid song about feelings from the 1970s, and we smoked and took off our clothes and, yes, had sex and he knew everything to do. I'd like to think he still feels me too.

But still, something tells me that, sooner or later, one of us is going to crack, and finally it happens.

"This is dumb," Andy says. "Can't we just talk?" He reaches over and slams my locker door shut so I can't hide behind it anymore. The hallway has emptied out, everyone else on their way home.

"About what?"

"I don't know. Anything. This is just…weird to pretend like we don't know each other."

"I have to catch the bus."

"My dad's picking me so we can drop you off."

"We don't know each other. Not really."

Andy sighs. "What do you mean?"

"You lied."

"About what?"

"You. About Minneapolis. That you already…had some-body."

Andy opens his mouth, like he's about to say something but at first nothing comes out but air. "How did you find out about that?"

"What's the difference? It's true, isn't it?"

"Does everybody know?"

I shrug my shoulders. "I have no idea. But I know."

He nods slowly, then flips his hair. The thing he always does when he's trying to look cool or he's nervous. "I was scared."

"Of me?"

"Sort of. And people finding out."

"Why would you be afraid of me?"

He looks past me, over my shoulder. "I was afraid that you'd stop being my friend. I didn't know anybody, I was all alone."

"You could have told me. If we were friends. But you didn't, so maybe we weren't friends after all."

"My parents would have killed me if I'd told. If people knew the real reason we came here, they'd—"

"Call you names? Welcome to the club." It comes out a little snotty, but I'm on a roll.

He sighs again. "Sorry, man." *Man* again. Andy the cool guy again, trying to talk his way out of it. "I know I should have just told you everything, but I thought I'd stopped being that way… and then I saw you that day in the shower, and then we started hanging out, and then we got high, and then…everything just started…coming out again. But I know it was wrong. I'm trying to fix it. I'm working really, really hard. I could fix it for the both of us. We could pray together, go to my church, and we would be all right. We could be friends again. We just wouldn't be able to, you know…"

"I don't want to be fixed."

But Andy doesn't hear me. "I just need…friends. Real ones."

"But I do too."

And with that, there's nothing more to say. We stand there, the only sound the custodian's floor polisher humming one hallway over. I open my locker again, the metal door now between us. Andy waits a moment, for something, and then closes his locker quietly and walks away, again. I watch him go, and hold on to the door to keep me in one place, until he's out of sight.

17

There's Been a Change in the Weather

"Need any help?"

When I get home I find my father kneeling in the brown, muddy grass, fixing the back gate yet again, the gate that's been opening and closing by itself and it's been driving him crazy trying to figure out why. "Hand me those pliers in the bottom drawer there," he says, pointing to his toolbox with one hand and holding the latch with the other.

I dig them out and hold them up. "These?"

"Yup." He tightens the bolts on the latch. "We'll see how this works. But what do you want to bet we'll come out here this time tomorrow and she'll be swinging wide open." To my father, everything on the farm—the tractor, the milking machines, pretty much anything that has a moving part—has always been a she. That, of course, made sense to me for the cows—they really are shes—but not for anything else. "It's a farmer thing," my mother had said when I asked her about it once. "I don't know how it got started. It doesn't matter if you've been a farmer since birth, or a recent convert, but every farmer talks that way. Nothing is ever a he." And my father is a farmer, no matter what anyone says about how he came to be one and why, and even though he could probably find some explanation for why calling inanimate objects using a female pronoun violated all sorts of rules of the English language.

"Ellen and your little sister back from town yet?" he asks. Even though it's nearly December, the sun beats down, and my neck and back are damp underneath my sweatshirt. Is that because it's still high in the sky, or is it low? Mr. Osterman told us once, even though we were studying rocks and not planets, adding that while he wasn't an expert, astronomy was an "avocation" of his, without bothering to define what that meant. That led Andy to comment to me under his breath that only a dipshit like Osterman would use his vacation to study something he didn't have to. I feel myself wanting to smile, thinking about it, because it's typical Andy, but then I put the brakes on it as fast as I can. I'm not ready to remember the good things quite yet until I've felt the bad first. It seems like that is how things are supposed to be, like you have to do them in the right order.

"Son? You off in outer space again?"

"What? No, they're not back yet."

"You doing homework?"

I shake my head.

My father stands up and brushes off his overalls. "You just sitting around the house, moping?"

"I'm not moping," I say, even though I must look like it, even just a little bit, for my father to have noticed.

"You could have fooled me," he says, folding up the drawers of the toolbox and latching it shut with a click. "Everything okay?"

"I guess," I say, even though it's a lie. I came out here looking for him because I thought it would help to tell somebody about what's just happened, and about what's been happening. Now I'm not so sure. Sooner or later I'll be telling Cathy about it, and while I'm not looking forward to rehashing it all, I have a feeling she'll know the right things to say. I know that she is going to be a good friend for a long time, and for that I'm glad.

I want my father to know about it too. To know something about me, something…important. But *important* doesn't even begin to describe it. It's everything. And if my mother were here, wouldn't I do the same thing? Yes. But I'd tell her first, and let her decide if I should say anything to my father. Let her run interference, protect me from his reaction if it was bad. But I don't have that option. He's all I have left in the parent department. He's here, now. And I want him to know.

To know me.

"Andy and I… We had another…"

What was the phrase my father has used before?

"Falling out?"

I nod.

He smiles and pats me on the shoulder. "You boys will work it out. Friendships are like that. One day you can't stand the sight of each other, then the next day you're inseparable."

"I don't think so. Not this time."

My father frowns. "What do you mean?"

And here it is: the chance to tell everything, about the picture, the pot, even what happened after that, what it all has felt like. And when that's done, my wanting to look for someone. The whole "another" thing. Is today, a warm Thursday in late November, the right time, the right day? To open the door, just a tiny bit? And if it doesn't go well, can I close it again? Bolt it shut, like the gate on the back of our property, so that nothing else about me can get out?

"I've decided to broaden my horizons," I say, borrowing the phrase from my father, which I had always thought was somewhat lame but I've now come to like. I like how it sounds, and I hope my father likes it too, hearing me use his language, out loud, following his advice. And what's more, I already have. No going back now. Or at least I'm going to try not to go back.

"Oh, that," he says. "I just meant that it wouldn't hurt to make friends with some of the other boys. You can still keep Andy."

"I know," I say. *But I can't keep him. I know that now. If I do, it's only going to hurt me.* "I just think it'd be better if I tried to find people who are more like me...broaden my horizons, like you said before." I haven't told him everything, I know, but it's a start.

My father smiles. "That phrase has made a real impression on you. But you can decide for yourself who you want to be with and who you don't. You don't need me to tell you what to do."

"You can if you want to," I say. "I don't mind."

"Don't worry, I will." He chuckles softly. "But you're going to get knocked around a bit no matter what I tell you. I can't save you from that. But you're strong. You've got a mind of your own."

"I do?" If I have to ask, I wonder if it can be really true.

"You're like your mother." And then he looks away, as if the sun is too bright for his eyes.

I'm not sure what else there is to say, but I'm not ready to leave him yet either. It seems like there's something else in the air, between us, and if I just stand quietly and watch him sort through his trays of screws and bolts, eventually he'll tell me. It feels like that kind of day.

"Warm day," my father says, after a few minutes. "Which means January will be more of a bear than usual." More typical farmer logic: beautiful weather must always be paid for by bad, to make sure everything stays in perfect alignment. My mother used to laugh about that too, saying that someday my father will wake up and find a bad summer (too hot, too dry, or too wet) followed by a miserable fall (snow in the middle of October), or a perfect April giving way to an even more perfect May and June. But when I think about it, I like that idea of balance; after bad times, like what happened with Andy, there has to be good to come. I'm counting on that.

The cows are scattered out in the pasture, nosing the brown grass, digging for some sign of green. Wind's coming in from the south, my father adds, and has been all fall, which is why we haven't had much snow yet. But in a few weeks it'll be Christmas, and my father says we're about due for a big snowstorm. Again, it's about taking the bad with the good. So far we've had barely enough snow to cover the ground in a gray, crusty sheet.

"How much do you think we'll get?" I ask.

"Oh, a foot at least," he says. "Or maybe even two." He smiles.

"Anna will like that." Already I can hear her begging for sled rides from the house to the barn and back again, pretending it's a one-horse open sleigh, with me playing the part of the horse. There were a lot of sled rides last winter, sometimes on the bare grass if the snow wouldn't cooperate. And when it was simply too muddy to do anything, Anna would cry and carry on, her wails of "I want sled!" usually followed by wails of wanting mother, until the two things sometimes got combined. What she wanted more than anything was her mother to come back and pull the sled like she had done the year before, when there was snow and there was a mother. I wanted that, too. But sooner or later she would settle down, we'd find some other game to play, or best of all the snow would finally come, and off we would go. In her own two-year-old way, she'd figured out what she needed to do to go on.

And as I stop and look up at the clear blue sky, hoping for snow, I know I'll figure out how to go on too.

"What are you looking at?"

"Nothing. I was just thinking about snow coming. I like the first couple of times, when it seems like it's new, like it's never happened before. But then we get used to it, and it's not special anymore."

My father looks up too, pulling his cap down a little bit to shield his eyes from the sun. "But isn't it nice to still be surprised? Even though you know how it's going to turn out in the end? It's like a surprise that you can count on, even though surprises aren't supposed to be that way."

Maybe I'd known all along how things would turn out with Andy, but it is nice to know that there might be somebody out there for me, because I can't ever imagine it happening. To have a surprise that didn't necessarily turn out the way you thought it would. Maybe that is supposed to be the good part to all of this, to know something is possible.

My father pulls off his cap, runs his fingers through his hair, and shakes his head a little bit, like he's trying to wake up. He looks tired, with small dark pockets under his eyes. Not old, but older. When did that happen? "I sort of had my own surprise the other day," he says, out of the blue.

"What do you mean?"

"We're keeping them."

"What?"

"The cows. This." He sweeps his arms out in front of him and then to the sides. "I made up my mind. I thought I wanted things to change, but I don't. You don't know how close I was. I was all set to sign on the dotted line, but I couldn't. Surprise." But he says it softly, like he's still not sure.

A cool breeze ruffles my hair, and I feel like it could lift me off the ground too. On the same day that everything I think about seems to hurt, something good is still happening. "What changed your mind?"

"You, mostly."

"Me?"

"I was worried that, if we kept going with the cows, you'd feel like you had to keep going too. You'd think that was what I wanted you to be. And I didn't want you to feel that way. So I thought I'd decide it for you by getting rid of them."

I nod but don't say anything.

"And I realized, during one of those nights after supper when I was driving around, trying to figure out what to do, that I needed to have a little more faith in you."

"Faith?"

"To decide for yourself what you wanted to be. Whether the cows are here or not. You're a smart guy and you can be whatever you want. Look at what I did. I'm being what I want. I finally figured that out. How I don't know, but I'm not going to question it. Am I making any sense at all?"

"I think so." I take a minute to run the whole thing through my head before I try it out. "Just because we have cows doesn't mean I have to be a dairy farmer. Is that it?"

"Pretty much."

"And it would be okay if I wanted them, but also okay if I didn't?"

"Bingo."

"But I thought it was more about the money."

My father takes a deep breath and lets it out slowly. "I won't kid you. We're just scraping by. But some things are more important than that. Doing what makes you happy. And letting your kids figure things out for themselves. Even Anna. She might not want to have anything to do with this place when she grows up. Or she might just take after her mother and corral some young man into taking over from me." He smiles again, and I realize he's trying to kid a little bit in the middle of all the seriousness, talking about the future and the next twenty years and beyond that. Our lifetimes.

I'm not sure I really get all of it, but I think I've got the main idea. "You can't decide things for people," I say. The son lecturing the father. *But I ought to know. I was trying to decide things for Andy.*

"That's what I figured out," he says. "You don't need me to decide your future. You need to do that. If you decide to be something else, you can do what I did. Decide yes, or no. You're a smart man. You'll know what to do. You'll have to trust me."

"I don't trust anyone right now."

"You can't let one person do that to you."

"You...know about...me. And about Andy and me." *There. Done.*

He laughs softly. "Yes, I suppose I do."

"How?"

My father smiles. "Fatherly intuition? If there is such a thing, I suppose that's it. I wondered for a long time if you even knew. But along came Andy, and for a while you were someone new. I was glad, though I worried about what was going to happen. I don't think Spud is doing that boy any favors with all that hell and damnation nonsense. Though I know they must have been worried after all that business in the Cities."

"You knew about that too?"

"It's a small town." He chuckles. "Things always come out sooner or later."

Now it's my turn to chuckle. "Like me."

"Yes, I suppose so."

We're both quiet for a moment, pretending we're looking at the door again, trying to figure out how to fix it. Finally my father breaks the silence. "You have to be who you're going to be. Sometimes it takes a while to figure that out. You're lucky that you're getting a head start. Me...well, I guess I'm a slow learner. I'm a dairy farmer. And you're..." He hesitates, so I finish it for him.

"Gay. And a dairy farmer too. I'm a gay dairy farmer."

We both laugh even though I'm not sure why it's funny. Maybe it just feels good to let go a little bit. But when we're done, all that we're left with is the quiet.

"I can't go back now," my father says. "You can't either." He closes up the toolbox and puts his cap back on. "And even if we wanted to, your mother isn't going to let us. No matter what, she's always going to have the last word."

I nod. "Yes, she will." And just like that, everything has changed. Again.

Back in the house, Anna and Ellen are waiting for us to sit down for supper. "You two looked like you were having a pretty serious talk out there," Ellen says.

"We were," I say. "But everything's okay. Mostly."

"I'm glad," she says. She probably knows the whole story, I think, and I'm happy about that, happy that she knows me. She's one of us, and while I can't imagine her leaving us, I know someday she will. Anna will grow up, and so will I. I try to put that thought out of my mind. She's here with us now. That's the most important thing.

My father and I wash up, and then we all say grace, just as we always do, as my mother used to lead us: *Come lord Jesus, be our guest, and let these gifts to us be blessed...* A favorite of my mother's, and we never miss it, even if we miss her. Church, she could take or leave, but prayers, she said, were more important anyway.

"Snow's coming, Anna," I say, as I put a few green beans on her plate.

She looks at me, her eyes wide. "When, Carl?"

"Soon," I say. "Be ready for a surprise."

She looks at me, puzzled for a moment, and then laughs. We all laugh too.

The four of us eat quietly, waiting for the weather. But until it comes, there will always be cows, and chores, and then supper.

ACKNOWLEDGEMENTS

Chapter One, "Milk," was previously published in slightly different form in *Callisto: A Queer Fiction Journal.* Chapter Nine, "More Than a Feeling," was previously published in slightly different form in the anthology *Queer Voices: Poetry, Prose, and Pride,* Minnesota Historical Society Press. Deep and heartfelt thanks to Jaynie Royal and Pam Van Dyk for their support and belief in my work and for welcoming me so warmly to the Regal House family of writers.

This novel went through many revisions over many years, and I'm grateful to Maureen Aitken, Paulette Alden, Pat Cumbie, Alison McGhee, and Jennifer Quam, wonderful friends and writers all, who provided me with essential feedback and support to guide me along the often bumpy path.

This novel could not have been written without the time and support provided by residencies at the Anderson Center, Arte Studio Ginestrelle, the Golden Apple Art Residency, the Hambidge Center, the Hawthornden Castle International Retreat for Writers, the Kimmel Harding Nelson Center for the Arts, the Millay Colony for the Arts, the Ragdale Foundation, the Tofte Lake Center, and the Virginia Center for the Creative Arts. The McKnight and Jerome Foundations as well as the Minnesota State Arts Board and the Loft Literary Center also provided essential support in the early stages of this project.

Thanks to Ron Falzone for reassuring me that the novel was closer to being done that I thought it was and for introducing me to Douglas Sirk.

Thanks to Julie Harris for four decades of support, friendship, and Scrabble.

Thanks to Jim Nepp for tenth-grade biology class, Varsity Band, and everything we've shared since.

And thanks, most of all and always, to Tom, for still being the guy the cat liked and for everything.